Tom Gallacher

JOURNEYMAN

Copyright © 1984 by Tom Gallacher.

First published in Great Britain in 1984 by Hamish Hamilton Ltd.

Sceptre edition 1987

Sceptre is an imprint of Hodder and Stoughton Paperbacks, a division of Hodder and Stoughton Ltd.

British Library C.I.P.

Gallacher, Tom
  Journeyman.
  I. Title
  823'.914[F]   PR6057.A388

  ISBN 0-340-40782-4

Printed and bound in Great Britain for Hodder and Stoughton Paperbacks, a division of Hodder and Stoughton Ltd., Mill Road, Dunton Green, Sevenoaks, Kent (Editorial Office: 47 Bedford Square, London, WC1B 3DP) by Richard Clay Ltd., Bungay, Suffolk. Photoset by Rowland Phototypesetting Ltd., Bury St Edmunds, Suffolk.

For the Udinese and the Genovese
who saw that language
was no barrier to affection

ONE

For reasons that I'm ashamed of now, I was living in Montreal in the spring of 1967 when Hugh Gillespie decided that he must find cheaper digs and arrived at Madame Girard's in the east end. Though his reasons for being there were much stranger than mine, I think neither of us would have chosen that city as an ideal place on which to balance such a pivotal year in our lives. For in Montreal they distrust the axiom that it's better to light a candle than curse the dark. They prefer to light a fuse and cheer the explosion.

It was entirely by chance that I was the first person Gillespie saw; though not the first person he *thought* he saw. The room he'd rented was being vacated by a friend of mine called Otto Maier and I was just standing there, looking out of the window, when I heard a sudden rush of footsteps and a new voice.

'Sam!'

I turned to face him. 'Pardon?' He'd stopped right in the centre of the room and his face shone with a mixture of joy and disbelief. That expression must have been generated by a hope which he was loath to abandon for, looking straight at me, he said the name again.

'Sam?'

'No.'

'Oh. Sorry. Thought it was somebody A knew,' he said. And not only did his expression fade but his face seemed to change – as did his voice and his manner. 'This is room five, is it no'? Whi' the hell are you up tae?'

I smiled. The combination of his strong Glasgow accent, and the defensive belligerence with which he used it, chimed in my memory. 'Yes, this is room five, and I am waiting for the man who's moving out.'

'A'm the man that's movin' *in*,' he challenged. It was as though nothing short of a full-blooded argument would camouflage that moment when he had so completely dropped his guard.

'Yes,' I said. 'I expect that's why you're here, but you're a little early.'

'An' you were even earlier! A think you'd better try for a room somewhere else, mister.'

This was pertinent but I told him, 'I already have a room, downstairs. I'll only be here a few minutes. I'd like to see Otto before he goes out with the other boarders for a farewell lunch.'

'Oh, aye? Otto. An' where the hell's *he*?'

'I think he's down the corridor in the lavatory.'

The Scotsman nodded as though this was the first plausible statement he'd heard from me. He looked around the room then went to retrieve his bags which his initial excitement had caused him to drop at the threshold.

'My name is Bill Thompson,' I said.

'Hugh Gillespie,' he replied without looking at me. 'Do you have any relations called Hanson?'

'No.'

Now he did give me a quick and comprehensive stare – presumably to detect if I was lying. He shook his head in irritated bewilderment and turned away again. 'You been here long?'

'Since October of last year.'

Gillespie dumped his baggage on a bed and gave all his attention to the room. The large double window overlooked St Catherine Street, or rue Ste-Catherine as it was plainly called this far east in the city. Drawn up by the window was the only armchair, an overstuffed, high-backed veteran which had at least three layers of stretch covers showing through at the busted corners. The other chairs were little more than collapsible camp-stools, parked on wide areas of bare linoleum. There were two single beds – one made and one stripped – which jutted in parallel from the long inner wall to the middle of the floor. They were separated by a door across which a metal bar was clamped to form an efficient barricade. In the middle of the wall by the door stood a tall, plum-coloured chest of drawers. Stacked beside it were Otto's already packed suitcase and bags. I was sitting on what looked like a child's desk as I watched the new tenant survey his domain. He asked, 'Is the food all right here?' rather as though he felt there must be *something* which would make up for the evident lack of comfort.

I was glad to give reassurance. 'Oh, yes. The food is excellent, and punctual. Who is Sam?'

'What?'

'You said "Sam" when you came into the room.'

'Did A?'

'Twice . . . to *me!*'

'So?' The belligerence was instantly available. 'A was mistakin'. Okay?'

'Sam . . . Hanson?'

'D'you know him?'

'No, but you mentioned the name Hanson and I assumed it must be the same person.'

He came strolling over. He was of middle height but heavy-looking. He confronted me, his shoulders hunched, angrily scratching his cheek with a stiff forefinger. 'Seems tae me you assume far too bloody much, Mr Thompson.'

Again a memory was alerted and I noted how close Scotsmen stand; even to a conversational adversary. I found myself copying the behaviour I'd seen others adopt many years before; not stepping back but *leaning* back a little from the hips. 'Maybe,' I said. 'And you are far too bloody touchy.'

It was then that Otto returned to collect his luggage. Gillespie's manner again changed, with that suddenness which I was to find so perplexing in the months that followed. To Otto he showed a warm and friendly demeanour and even came close to apologising for the fact of his being there too soon. Moreover, he took the trouble to iron out the less comprehensible aspects of his accent when talking to the German – though Otto spoke excellent English. I left them chatting together and busied myself carrying the outgoing luggage down to the car. I was helped by my fellow boarders; by Paul who was the owner of the car, Carlo his fellow Italian, and Emile who was the strongest of the three but content merely to supervise the loading.

They made it clear that they were offended by my decision not to join the lunch party, although they did not refer to it. Considering what good times we'd all had together during the winter and, in particular, how friendly Otto and I had been, this new evidence of my recently strange behaviour must have seemed to them very sad and, no doubt, *petty*.

Otto himself, when he managed to tear himself away from the charming Scotsman, was less affected by the odd circumstances. 'This new guy is a very pleasant fellow,' he said.

'Really?'

'Did you not think so?'

'No, I didn't.'

'You must not expect so much of people, Bill. Not anyway in their crisis year.'

The others were now seated in the car. I caught Otto's arm as he turned to join them. 'Is he? Did you ask him if he was twenty-seven?'

'I do not need to ask.'

Paul started the engine of the large green Oldsmobile and the car radio came on. The singer was instantly identifiable. Otto smiled and made a gesture towards the music, as though some proof of his assertion had been conjured out of the ether. We had often discussed his theory that between the ages of twenty-six and twenty-eight men reach a decisive moment in their lives which governs everything they subsequently do. It was mainly because of his belief in this theory that he was now on his way to San Francisco. In a few months his twenty-eighth year would begin and he wanted it to begin in the most fruitful circumstances that could be arranged. We shook hands and I wished him well. The car door slammed, cutting off the singer (also aged twenty-seven) who was inviting his tambourine man to play a song for him. It seemed to be aimed directly at Otto, for whom 'the jingle-jangle morning' had ineluctably arrived.

*   *   *

The dining-room of the boarding-house was on the first floor at the end of a long gloomy hallway which stretched from the front to the back of the house. In fact, it was merely a widened section of that hallway which, at lunch-time on Saturday, still smelt of the joss-sticks which the landlady burned every morning to aid her meditation. But it was only on Saturday that she prepared lunch for her boarders. On working days the meals were break-fast and dinner. On Sundays no meals were provided. Her name was Girard and she spoke only French or, more precisely, Québécois. She was a rather plump, terribly languid widow in her early fifties with huge dark eyes which drooped markedly at the outer corners. She never wore stockings indoors and, on her feet, always open-backed slippers in which she shuffled more than walked between her kitchen and the table. Her chief assistant and factotum was her teenage son, Jean-Pierre.

Having been told of the farewell outing for her German lodger, Madame Girard had set only one place – for Gillespie – at the table. He was already seated there. When she heard my foot-steps at the far end of the hallway she peered down its length then heaved a despairing sigh before unloading another set of plates and cutlery from the sideboard. I waited while she established another place, at Gillespie's elbow. He managed to hold silence while the side-salad was delivered and even during the preliminary skirmish of our attack on the chicken, but by then he had decided on his opening line. 'A wonder what Otto an' his friends are eatin'?'

'Something exotic, I expect.'

'Or Italian.'

'Or both.'

'Would you no' have liked that?' he asked, sliding the salad bowl towards me. I hadn't taken any, nor did I intend to.

I fended off the bowl, 'No, thank you.'

'Did you no' get on wi' Otto?'

'Yes, I did. Very well.'

'No' well enough to see him away, though?'

'I don't go out much during the day,' I said, and tried to make it sound as though that was the end of the matter. Yet it seemed the new lodger was willing to try calmness instead of bluster, so I did my bit in that direction. 'Have you just arrived in Montreal?'

'No. Been here a couple o' months. A had a flat, near the Mount.'

'Are you working in the city?'

'Hope tae. A'm a journalist. Came ower to cover the World fair.'

'I see. I'd have thought too much has been written about that already. Even when I arrived the papers were full of Expo '67.'

'That was in October, you said. That ye arrived?'

I nodded.

'From England?'

'Indirectly, yes.'

'But ye came directly here, tae this dump.'

Again I nodded and bent attentively over my plate, hoping to ward off further questions. It was Otto, I recalled, who'd been the first person *I* met when I arrived. But I had not chosen this particular house. It just happened to be known to the taxi driver I hailed in the west end of the city. My instruction was to drive as far east as one could reasonably hope to find lodgings. When I got out of the cab it seemed to me he'd pushed that commission to its limit. We were at a point where St Catherine Street borders the river wharves; an area where the tenements were old and high and more than a little decayed. In the dusk the driver pointed out a doorway. He told me to go up to the first floor and ask for Madame Girard. I met Otto halfway up the stairs. I told him my business and he, very helpfully, came back up with me to make sure there was a vacancy and to act as interpreter. Even so, there was some difficulty. Otto – who was a modern languages teacher – spoke the French of France whereas Madame Girard spoke only Québécois. But it was established that I would take a room for a week to enable me to find a flat elsewhere. For thirty-five dollars, in advance, I could have half-board. I handed over the money and started to unpack. Curiously, Otto remained in attendance and apparently had forgotten that he'd been going out when I came in and, presumably, had somewhere to go. He'd hovered at the open door, watching me unpack. It occurred to me as not unlikely that I'd been neatly delivered by the taxi driver to be fleeced by this German who'd been lying in wait for easy pickings. Now, six months later, the sheer incongruity of that suspicion prompted me to take a more understanding view of Hugh Gillespie's evident suspicion of me. I offered a token remark to bridge the silence. 'So many people have written so much about Expo already.'

'But only about the expense; the massive bloody extravagance o' it. That's no' what interests me. They've got money all right. They've got plenty o' money, but by God they've got guts as well.' He picked up the remainder of his chicken by the bone for a direct attack and his voice climbed a couple of notches in genuine enthusiasm. 'What strikes *me* is the thought o' this whole violent city gatherin' for *the* most tremendous flyer . . . boostin' itself into Mecca. An' building a whole island in the St Lawrence tae do it! Impossible! Diggin' a complete new underground system tae do it – wi' every station a work of art. And why?' Gillespie paused to wring an equal response from me, but I had long ago used up what small interest I'd had in Expo '67. He answered his own question. 'So that four thousand people can reach wonderland every hour . . . eighteen hours a day . . . for six months! *Millions*!'

I felt bound to enter a slight cavil. 'But a lot of people will go several times, so the actual . . .'

Gillespie ignored it. 'An' for every one o' the millions – every solitary person – there will be somethin' special that happens. Maybe a small thing: a smell, a view, a feelin', a state o' mind.' His voice dropped for more effective emphasis. 'Somebody in the crowd. But somethin' that happens once in a lifetime . . . and it's happenin' *here*.'

'Is Mayor Drapeau paying you to say all this?'

'Somebody'll have tae, because that's what A want to write about. Montreal this summer is a state of mind.' He reclaimed the salad bowl and tipped the liquid residue over the remnants on his plate. 'I'm a freelance writer. A'm hopin' tae line up a man-on-the-spot deal with some UK papers.'

'Oh?' I tried to sound no more than politely interested, but

16   TOM GALLACHER

clearly my safety in Montreal might be threatened by a man bent on getting too accurate a shade of local colour.

Apparently I'd betrayed more than polite interest. 'What's wrong?'

'Nothing. But I suppose you'll just be dealing with the city in general and the Expo site, won't you?'

'What dae ye mean, "*just*"?'

I laughed uneasily. 'Well, you would scarcely want to do an article on Madame Girard!'

'Or you?'

'Or any of us here.' I fidgeted under his close-range and amused stare.

'But you in particular?'

It was then that Madame Girard's son, Jean-Pierre, came bustling in, laden with groceries.

'Excuse me.' I stood up abruptly and started back down the long hallway. Almost at the door of my room I remembered the ritual. '*Merci, Madame,*' I called.

Wearily but unseen in the kitchen the lady responded, '*Bienvenue!*'

My room was on the same floor as the dining-room. It was equipped with a television set, and an air-conditioning unit which blocked out and protruded beyond the lower third of the tall narrow window. These refinements, plus a carpet and a 'compact' sitting-room suite, indicated that I had one of the best rooms in the house. Together with meals it cost me thirty-five dollars a week.

When I'd arrived that had seemed a reasonable charge, but now it was becoming an alarming drain on my savings. I wished that I'd taken a job during the winter. That, surely, would have been safe enough. Even as part of the nomadic army of snow-clearers I could have built up my reserve of cash. As I lay on my bed digesting the Saturday lunch, I felt angry with myself, recalling with what complacency I'd gone to ground in Montreal at the glowing, treacly-humid end of the Indian summer. And, not much later, with what satisfaction I'd stood at the tall window, willing the first snowflakes to fall faster and thicker knowing that, with such evidence here, blizzards would also be sweeping across the great lakes; blanketing the low hills of Duluth at the western end of Superior; covering my notional tracks through Huron, Erie and Ontario from which the last ocean-going ships of the year must have long gone, to escape into the Gulf of St Lawrence and the Atlantic. Then, for months on end, the ice had gathered round the island city as an impenetrable barrier. I listened gleefully to the almost hourly radio reports of the falling temperature and imagined my crystalline defence force creeping eastward and outward from me, erecting fortifications at Lachine, then Trois Rivières and finally Quebec.

Now, one by one, all those defences were falling again. In recent weeks when the traffic noise had abated in the early hours of the morning, I'd been brought fearfully awake by ragged detonations as huge stretches of ice broke apart in mile-wide cracks. And whereas there was still a lot of snow on the streets, the ice on the river melted much faster than it had frozen. There was a loud tap at the door and I levered myself up on my elbows. 'Yes?'

Madame Girard's son and helper, Jean-Pierre, edged into the room. He was a scrawny-looking boy of seventeen with greasy dark hair. His voice had a permanent whine and he spoke both English and French with a strong Canadian accent. 'About the room upstairs,' he began, 'my mother says she's sorry but she had to let it go to that new guy.'

'That's all right. Maybe I could have the next one that falls vacant.'

Jean-Pierre shrugged doubtfully. 'Maybe.' Both he and his mother knew that there was no virtue in letting a thirty-five-dollar boarder become a twenty-five-dollar boarder when the best room in the house was always the hardest to let. The shrug slid easily into a concerned, slow head shaking. 'Let me tell ya, I don't think you'd be comfortable up there.'

'Why not?'

Jean-Pierre advanced into the room, looking around as though freshly amazed at the prodigal variety of the furnishings. 'Well, look what you've got here! Upstairs, everything's a whole lot more . . .' he brought out a newly acquired word '. . . functional.'

'And a lot cheaper,' I observed crassly.

'Not for much longer.' Jean-Pierre sighed in a manner he hadn't practised well enough and sat down on the end of the bed as though a crushing burden of responsibility had suddenly been placed on his young shoulders. 'All the rents will have to go up now.'

'Oh?' I felt a slight but sickening ache gather in my chest.

'Expo!' The landlady's son spread his arms theatrically. There was, in all his dealings with the boarders, that air of under-rehearsed pretence; as though these paying guests were no more than lay figures in his essential training as a confidence trickster. It did not seem to matter if he convinced them or not, as long as he made some progress in his vocation. 'Have you any idea what American tourists will want to pay for accommodation like this?'

Though incredulous at the effrontery, it was a point worth pushing. 'I can imagine this might be just what they're looking for,' I lied, 'but that's a good reason for getting all of us onto the top floor, isn't it? To make these rooms available.'

'They'll want the rooms on the top floor as well,' Jean-Pierre whined in dismay. 'There'll be no fighting them off once Expo opens.'

I felt that some cool reason would mitigate the anguish Madame Girard must have faced in deciding to increase her rents. 'We are very far east of Expo,' I said. 'Maybe too far to be convenient for Americans.'

'They won't know how far it is when they book.' That stark observation slipped out unadorned, and young Girard realised that no further progress could be made by adding to his rent-rise performance at that moment. He rose abruptly and devoted some attention to his other major role as chief snooper of the household. He ambled over to my dressing-table which served mainly as a desk. Of course he'd already seen all that was to be seen when I was out. He rattled the space-bar of my portable typewriter until the bell rang. 'How's the writing coming along?'

My reply came through gritted teeth. 'Not very well.'

Jean-Pierre turned suddenly to face me; jolting some lank strands of hair out of place. 'You must type very quiet, you know that?'

'What?'

'How'd you manage that? Typing so quiet? We hardly ever hear ya doing it.'

'I try not to disturb anyone.'

'New guy's got a typewriter.'

'I expect he has.'

'Why's that?' This was Jean-Pierre's verbal reflex. Sometimes he snapped it out as a surprise question but most often as a general-purpose, on-the-ball, alert signal.

'He tells me he's a journalist,' I replied.

'That's what he tells me, too.'

'Then I expect he is.'

Jean-Pierre gave a little cough of a laugh in salute of my naivety. 'Then how come he has to pay to put in an ad? Newspaper called him on our number to check out his new address.'

'Which paper?'

'English, natural. The *Star*. I give them the number of the 'phone upstairs to call.'

'But surely you could have confirmed the address!'

He spread his hands. 'It's not my business,' he said, and gave his attention to *my* business. He wandered to the small table by the armchair on which were several thick notebooks. 'You're not in newspapers, though? I mean that's not the kinda writing you do.'

'No. I'm writing a book.'

'Another book.'

I tried to remember which particular lies I'd told Jean-Pierre on earlier occasions; aware that the youth probably knew they were lies and had infinitely better recall. 'Yes,' I murmured vaguely.

'Why's that?'

'Pardon?'

'You finish the other one?'

'Which one was that?'

'How many books you written, Bill?' the youth chuckled – and again gave the impression that somebody had taught him how to do it; together with suggestions on what posture to adopt while chuckling. Failing an answer from me, Jean-Pierre picked up one of the notebooks and started leafing through it – as though for the first time. 'I guess it takes a lot of working out before you get down to typing it.'

'Yes, it does.'

My interrogator skipped through a number of entries that had been made many years earlier and alluded to a recurring place name. 'Where *is* Greenock?'

'In Scotland.'

'The new guy is from Scotland.'

'So I believe.'

'Maybe he could help you with your new book.'

'I shouldn't think so. There's no difficulty about remembering Scotland.'

Jean-Pierre slammed the notebook back on the table. 'How come,' he asked, 'you don't answer the door when you're right here? You been sick?'

I tried to maintain the slightly bored and casual manner. 'When was this?'

'Lotsa times, when some Joe comes to see you, my mother pounds on your door but you don't show. Why's that?'

'I'm busy. I just don't want to see anybody.'

'Well – it's your business, mister, but . . .'

'Yes, it is.' I swung to my feet to the floor with such alacrity that Jean-Pierre backed away a couple of paces.

'Yeah. Well's I said, my mother's sorry about the room upstairs.'

'Okay!'

Jean-Pierre gave a quick nod and a smile before he turned to leave. I heard him go, whistling flat, along the hallway to his own room. Obviously he was pleased with the interview; and I could guess why. It was now clear to him that I was hiding. That meant somebody must be looking for me. And *that* meant somebody might pay to discover where I could be found. Jean-Pierre went to his room mentally juggling a negotiable nugget of information. But he had also parted with just such a nugget.

I cleared away some notes from the armchair and fished out the *Montreal Star*. If the newspaper wanted to check on the new address of an advertiser then his advertisement must be currently running. I found it in the Personal column. It did not surprise me that Hugh Gillespie had achieved a masterly economy in his message. What was surprising was the lack of bait. It read: 'Sam Hanson, brother of Donny – do not leave Montreal without contacting this box.'

Why, I wondered, had he gone to the extra expense of a box number and yet had not offered any inducement at all for Sam Hanson to pursue the request? Apart from that, I had to revise my initial understanding of the situation. When Gillespie had burst in upon me, my reading of the event was that he'd expected to find the other person there. He had, I thought, already arranged the meeting with someone he knew to be in Montreal. But clearly that was not so. He did not know where Sam Hanson was. That blaze of exultation which had been mistakenly directed at me had no stronger basis than a two-line advertisement buried in columns of newsprint.

I laid down the newspaper and stared up at the ceiling, whose cracks were strongly defined by the reflection from the snow which still lay in the street. I nodded at the clumsy repair work and knew for a fact that, whatever he might say, the real reason that Gillespie had come to this city was to find Sam Hanson.

TWO

It was my habit now to sleep very late on Sundays. It delayed the hunger. And when I did get up I spent as long as possible bathing and shaving and dressing. Not until then did I take the first of the cheese biscuits which, together with a few cans of 7-Up, were to sustain me through the day. When first I'd adopted self-imposed seclusion, the regime of one day of fasting a week was aimed at solving several difficulties. It kept me out of sight, it saved money and – I'd convinced myself – it would stimulate whatever creative ability I possessed. And that was true. What I'd overlooked was the more basic fact that fasting makes you miserable, hungry and tired. In that condition, no matter how stimulated my creative ability might be, it failed for lack of energy. All that was produced was a further accumulation of notes which maddeningly failed to join up with the material in my old Greenock notebooks.

Though Sussex born and bred, I had served my marine engineering apprenticeship in a Clydeside shipyard. And *that* was my father's idea, too. My father believed the success of his engineering consultants company owed everything to his own Clydeside apprenticeship. So I was sent to Greenock at the age of sixteen and lodged there for five years. During that time I gradually filled several notebooks with information about the people I met and their way of life. I noted the facts of their character and situation quite impartially and was no less critical of my own foolishness with regard to them than I was of their often extravagant thoughtlessness.

But the events and characters remained as separate events and characters. After six months of constant chivvying they still refused to come together as a novel; and obviously, unless I could turn them into a novel they were quite useless. Sunk in my armchair I glanced ruefully at the piles of paper by my side. There were many pages which started off bravely typed but soon petered out into scrawled long-hand. And the new notes were now more than double the volume of those old notebooks which for the last six years I'd ferried hopefully across oceans; dog-eared tallymen of their own, as well as my, expectations.

It was not that I enjoyed being a sea-going engineer. Shuttling back and forward in a noisy, heaving, hot steel box has little to commend it. When I was freshly out of my apprenticeship, the life of a journeyman afloat had promised to be full of colour and excitement and adventure in foreign ports. I had embarked on a cargo vessel firmly believing that its ports of call must be identical with those of a passenger cruiser. In fact it was only sometimes that they even went to the same *countries*. In the main, the harbours and ports at which cargo vessels called fell into two categories; they were hot or they were cold. The hot ones were barren and flat and miles from civilisation. The cold ones were wet as well and pitched in the heart of huge industrial enclaves, closed in by blank warehouse walls and circled as far as the eye could see by railway sidings.

Even in those places, of course, it was possible to get away from the ship. Only an exorbitant taxi ride away there were always small smoky drinking dens and at least one grimy-windowed whorehouse which didn't need windows at all. And on a few occasions I did set out in a packed taxi to prove myself equal to the joys and hazards of the wild seafaring life. Then later, with my shipmates, I joined in the boasting at how joyfully we had overcome the rough necessities offered. That was the best part of it. Back on the clean, well-oiled, ship I realised that the real pleasure of going ashore was the talking about it afterwards. Nobody had found a better way to prove what men we were. And nobody questioned whether or not such proof was needed, nor by whom.

I lifted the pile of notes from the carpet and dumped them in my lap. What *they* proved was the difference between a writer and a person who wants to write. And why was it, I wondered, that even these new notes, written at leisure and with great care in whole empty days devoted to nothing else, were much less interesting to read than the hastily scribbled entries in the old notebooks by a grimy-fingered apprentice in random minutes at work. I reached to the other side of the chair and brought up the packet of cheese biscuits. I took out a ration of three in the hope of pacifying my mutinous stomach. As I crunched on the dry but sustaining morsels the crumbs fell on several pages, all of which were headed 'Chapter One'.

In the afternoon I was weary enough to sleep again. I woke at the sound of laughter on the stair and immediately felt desperately hungry. The spring daylight was already beginning to fade and from the window I saw Paul and Carlo jostling each other onto the sidewalk as they set off to have dinner together. Carlo was laughing at something Paul had said. It occurred to me that that was perhaps the only advantage of becoming a recluse – my friends did not feel bound to speak English and therefore Carlo was not excluded from the conversation. Even so, I was tempted to pull on my jacket and go after them; to squander a week's careful budgeting on a good meal. My stomach thought the only danger was emptiness. I leaned to the side of the window watching my fellow boarders recede jauntily under the glow of neon signs on the many restaurant frontages. They were doing what they wanted to do, with the full approval of their families. Tomorrow they would go to jobs they enjoyed working at. And they lived in this depressing house not because they had to but because they wanted to save money or send it home. I gritted my teeth in the current of warm air rising from the radiator. If my family needed only money sent to them, how much simpler life would be. But they had enough money of their own. They had enough everything of their own.

Turning from the window I found the room was quite dark. My stomach groaned and sent a series of stabbing reminders all over my body. I switched on the table lamp which had the violent yellow shade and sat down at the dressing-table/desk which was too high to provide a comfortable position for writing. I placed a fresh sheet of paper in front of me, ruled two rough columns, and for the umpteenth time started jotting down the foreseeable expenses against the current balance. On the result of that calculation I worked out the latest estimate of the time I had left before I must give myself up. Assuming no increase of rent and board, and nothing but hungry Sundays, I could remain a fugitive until mid-July. I was determined that I must have those three more months, at least. By then, surely, I'd be able to prove that what I could write was worth . . .

There was a loud knock on my door. 'Come in!' I called. It was the young French boarder, Emile, who came in. He stood almost apologetically in the shadow by the door.

'Will you come with us to have dinner?' he said, as though he had not made that suggestion several times before and been refused.

'But Paul and Carlo have already gone out.'

'Yes, I know. I mean with the new guy and me. He is waiting and I told him I would show him the place where you go for the terrible English food. I mean the place where you used to go.' He grinned as though to disarm anticipated impatience. 'He says he would like to stand both of us dinner. I think that means he will pay.'

'That's what it means,' I said, and tried to get to my feet without displaying undue eagerness. 'Let's go.'

Gillespie was waiting in the dusk of the landing and when he saw that I was following Emile out he merely nodded and started immediately downstairs. It struck me as I watched his stocky jolting figure silhouetted against the street entrance that he could not want my company for any other reason than to gather information. But probably Emile suggested that I should come along.

Since it was the general practice for landladies to take all of Sunday off, the streets in the east end were soon thronged with hungry boarders. Now was the high point of the week for the restaurants and cafés for miles around. It started at breakfast, increased at lunch but reached a peak of activity for the main meal on Sunday evening.

We descended to the sidewalk which was wet from the gradual

oozing of the melting snow margins, and threatening to freeze again. All along the block, east and west, other young men were emerging in twos and threes. And those already strolling to their favoured eating places were also strolling two by two. There were no groups of more than three, there were no single persons and certainly there were no young women to be seen. I shrugged the collar of my jerkin higher around my neck against the breeze and tried to get a reassuring message through to my stomach which was violently stimulated by the sharp freshness of the open air. We passed a number of cafés with juke boxes blaring but on quiet stretches there was only the purposeful tramp of feet and, from higher up the hill, several separate church bells sounding the angelus.

'This is the place,' said Emile and led us into a small restaurant. What it lacked in lighting it more than made up for in mirrors. Every possible surface was covered with tinted, faceted, curved or mosaic mirrors.

When the instant and invariable delivery of iced water had been accomplished and Gillespie had given our order, he looked around as though expecting to see someone he might know. 'Nothin' but reflections,' he grunted.

Emile nodded. 'That is so that people, looking in, will think the place is crowded.'

'Would that no' drive customers *away*?'

'No, no. That will mean it is a very popular restaurant – so the food must be good.'

'But you said it was mainly British people that came here. They don't want tae sit in a crowded restaurant – even if the food *is* good.' He glanced at me and I nodded in agreement.

Emile sighed and smiled. 'Ahhh!' It always delighted him when he came across such insights. He leaned stagily over the narrow table and confided, 'I think the owner does not know this.' His voice was solemn but his brown eyes had a mischievous glint which commented impartially on the fallible proprietor and the oddness of the British who judge restaurants not by the food they swallow but by the space around them while they do it.

'This is your usual place, is it?' Gillespie asked me.

'Yes. But it's a while since I've been here.'

'Nearly a month,' Emile irritated me by reporting. And no doubt he had reported other things to the new man on the top floor; though not anything he had been told in confidence. Unfortunately I had not stipulated that the lies I'd told Emile and the others were confidential. And it was the main strand of these which Gillespie now picked upon.

'You're in Montreal tae research a book, A believe.'

'Yes.'

'What's it about?'

Of course he would ask that. Naturally he would ask that. It was without doubt the very next question. And how could I say 'Greenock' to a Scotsman without arousing incredulity and suspicion? I pressed my lips together as though suppressing wind and in the pause tried to think of a possible subject which would be relevant to Montreal and yet distant enough from the truth. 'Indians,' I said. 'The Red Indians. I've always been fascinated by them.' I glanced at Emile and to my relief, and his great credit, he did not even blink, although it was wildly different from what I'd told him.

The food arrived and put off any detailed pursuit of the subject. As I leaned back to let the waitress load the table I reflected gratefully that the unvarying choice of British diners usually ensures quick service. And their way of eating usually precludes conversation. Certainly Gillespie ate as though the mechanics of it made him deaf. Emile tried once or twice to re-start the conversation without avail, but it was to him that the new man turned when the main trencher-work was done. 'And what do you do, Emile?'

'While the seaway is open, I work on the docks. In the winter, I work at anything I can do.'

Gillespie clattered his knife and fork onto the empty plate. 'Ye're a labourer.'

Before the Frenchman could reply I protested, 'You don't have to be so offensive about it.'

They both looked at me, surprised by the angry tone of my voice. Gillespie pushed with the heels of his hands against the table edge and the expression in his eyes shifted quickly to hostility. 'Mister,' he said, 'bein' a labourer might be an offensive thing tae you, but tae me it's jist a job.'

Emile, puzzled by the sudden chill in the atmosphere, smiled and shrugged, 'Yes. That is the job I do.'

I ignored his mediation and continued to stare at Gillespie. 'What is offensive,' I told him, 'is your assuming that if he works as a labourer he can't be very intelligent . . . or . . .' I floundered '. . . *valuable*. And he is. You'll find he is very intelligent, perceptive and valuable.'

'What makes ye think A don't know that, already?' the Scotsman asked, and it was clear he was making some effort to keep his own temper in check. 'What makes ye think A don't know a bloody sight mair aboot labourers, and men, than you?'

It was obvious to me that I'd made a serious mistake. Even so, it did not bother me that I might owe Gillespie an apology. I did have the sudden mortifying awareness that my mistaken defence of young Emile had done nothing but patronise *him*. Yet it was he who rescued himself and me from the widening chasm of embarrassment. 'Next time I do some labour,' he mused expansively, 'I want the rate for the job, sure. But also, I want bonus for being such a great guy.'

Gillespie and I both smiled and, over coffee, the talk turned to other things. First to the imminent increase in rent. Apparently Jean-Pierre had told them that there would be an increase of ten dollars, starting the following week and coinciding with the official opening of Expo '67. My brain raced through the well-rehearsed calculations again. Another ten dollars a week would cut my remaining time by a month. That would bring the crunch day to the end of June; and perhaps earlier, for other prices would be rising to celebrate the lucrative event of Expo. But I was damned if I'd let my whole future life be decided by ten dollars a week now. Also, I was anxious not to show the sickening sense of frustration the news gave me. Slowly I took another sip from my empty cup and remarked, 'In that case it's probably just as well that I'll be moving to another place.'

Emile was astonished. 'Bill! Are you?'

'Yes. The Girard's is too far away from the libraries and the books I need.'

'Always has been, A should think,' said Gillespie pointedly. He was bending forward, reaching into his jacket which hung over the back of his chair. His image was fractured by the mirrored hexagonal pillar behind him. The tinting of the glass gave his thin sandy hair an almost tangerine shade and enhanced his sallow complexion. As I watched him fish out a packet of cigarettes I tried to decide why he seemed to go out of his way to be objectionable. Becoming aware of my rather vacant look he went on, 'Pity A didnae meet you sooner. We could have swopped places. The flat A've jist left is bang in the middle o' the libraries. And the libraries are full o' WASPS.'

Emile was puzzled. 'Wasp. That is a sort of bee?'

Gillespie chuckled. 'Aye. A sort of bastard, right enough.'

'He means White Anglo-Saxon Protestants,' I explained.

'Ah! There are not many of them this far east in Montreal.'

'An' those there are keep quiet about it, eh?' He gave me a challenging look.

I responded, 'So – you're a refugee from religious persecution, Gillespie?'

'Hugh,' he said. 'My name is Hugh. Your public school manners are showin'.'

'I'm glad *some*body's manners are showing. But what makes you think I went to a public school?'

He grinned. 'Easy. First, the accent; though there's many a yobbo can imitate that well enough. The clincher is, you look that bloody *clean*! As though ye've had a bath every day of yer life from the day ye were born. Am A right?'

My irritation ignored caution as I retorted, 'Yes, except for five years in Greenock where there was no bathroom.' I regretted it instantly.

He blew out a long streamer of smoke. 'Greenock? An' what kinda Indians were ye doin' research on in Greenock?'

Emile, seeing or sensing my discomfiture, stood up abruptly. 'I think we should go for a walk now, before it is too cold in the air.'

'A good idea,' I said, then rearranged my expression to thank Gillespie. 'Thank you very much for the meal. I thoroughly enjoyed it.'

He nodded and signalled the waitress who was eager to secure our table for the second or third shift of boarders. But as he unravelled dollar bills onto the plate he observed, 'Five years. What could keep you that long withoot a bath, A wonder?'

Our French colleague showed signs of exasperation at this pursuit of what seemed to him occult trivialities. 'Are we going to walk or do we all go now to have a bath?'

'We walk,' said Gillespie.

Emile strode out of the restaurant at a pace he intended we should maintain, west on St Catherine then turning uphill on the broad, tree-lined avenue of Pie IX. And he was young and athletic enough to keep several steps ahead of us even when we came to the steeper bit. Gillespie and I trudged along for the most part in silence. If it hadn't been that I thought I was in some way showing appreciation for the free dinner I'd probably have gone straight back to the digs. But in that event I would have missed the first real clue to the private dream that Hugh Gillespie hoped to recapture in Montreal.

The street lights on Pie IX were entirely for motorists and strung on wires over the centre of the wide road, leaving the sidewalks in deep shadow. That and the fact that our walking abreast denied us any kind of duelling stance seemed to persuade the Scotsman he had defences enough to afford civility. Even so, he did not begin well. 'It's no' that I've taken a scunner tae you, Bill. A mean, you in particular. It's jist that A don't like Englishmen, in general.'

Since he gave no hint that I might prove an exception to this rule, I did not abase myself in gratitude.

He went on, 'It's jist a reflex, y'know. Everything we were taught at school was aimed at provin' the English were superior tae us and damn near every other country on God's earth. That breeds a kinda . . .' he sighed.

'Scepticism?'

'Aye.' He gave a grunt of laughter. 'At least! An' that's a good example. "Scepticism" is a sort o' word A would *write*, but A wouldnae say.'

Which clarified another doubt I'd had about Gillespie. I'd wondered at what sort of journalism he'd managed to make a living, given his manner of speech. But apparently he did not write the way he spoke. Later, I was able to confirm that he wrote like an Englishman. And an Englishman possessed of unnatural vitality, at that. 'I think you should use whatever word occurs to you,' I said.

'Sure. But the word that occurs tae me aboot you is, "liar".'

I stopped walking. Then so did he. Emile, unaware that we'd stopped forged even further ahead and merged into the fog which was gathering on the higher ground. My first instinct was to agree. A sense of guilt had been accumulating over the ease with which I now told lies.

But my accuser forestalled me. 'Of course, maybe ye've got good reasons for doin' it.'

'Maybe better reasons than you,' I said.

'A doubt it.' He inclined his head sharply ahead and we resumed our walk as mutually confessed but tacitly accepted liars. 'What dae *you* think A've been lyin' aboot?'

'The same as me, really. Your reason for being here.'

'Uh-huh?'

'Writing features about Expo is just a cover. All you actually want here is to find a particular person.'

'A very particular person.'

'Why?'

Gillespie's tone indicated that he was now almost eager to say what he was about to say and the curious vulnerability which I'd heard only once before was back in his voice. 'I've got tae find that person,' he said, 'because he is my witness.'

My mind was alerted only to some vague recollection that Hemingway had written about the need or pursuit of a 'witness'. And Gillespie did strike me as the sort of person who would enjoy reading Hemingway. I mentioned the name.

He disagreed. 'No, no. Got the idea fae somebody a bit further back than that. Pliny. The Younger, admittedly, but still a good way back.'

I was no longer so foolish as to express surprise that a tough, working-class Glasgow man should be familiar with a Latin commentator. I'd met too many Scots imbued with a ferocious zeal for self-education. 'And what did young Pliny say?' I asked.

'It was when somebody had died.' Gillespie adjusted his voice to do justice to the quote. 'He did not say "Christ Almighty, then I'm lost!" or even "Dearie me, how sad." Not at all. Pliny said, "I have lost the witness of my life. I fear I may henceforth live more carelessly".'

We'd taken a dozen paces in silence before the naked sincerity with which the essential lines were delivered had ebbed enough for me to observe, 'That was a very fine thing to say.'

'An', b'God, a true thing,' my companion growled.

There now approached us out of the mist an enormous grey bird which rapidly coalesced into its constituent parts as Emile and the two Italians linked line abreast with their arms on each other's shoulders. They were in high spirits. Gillespie and I were engulfed in the wings and hustled back down the hill. Apparently Paul and Carlo had decided on the same walk after dinner, but in the opposite direction – going east and up Viau before swinging back along Sherbrooke. They horsed around a good deal on the way back to the digs. Gillespie entered immediately into the prevailing mood and promised that he would, indeed, break out the beer he'd already stocked up. My mood did not re-adjust as quickly. I felt a keen foreboding of loss and – though carried along in the jostling, pummelling phalanx – feared that we, who were all strangers in that city, would become strangers everywhere because of the time we spent in Montreal. Probably the fear was no more than a heightening of my own uncertainty, depleted time, and now the necessity of renting still cheaper lodgings. But to the uneasiness of these was added the startling idea which Gillespie had uncovered. Where was *my* witness, that I had never sought to find or, having found, to keep? The chill fog gathered densely behind us, pulling itself forward on snaky tendrils through the bare branches and hovering like a grey wave above our heads by the time we reached the familiar corner of Pie IX and St Catherine East.

THREE

The business of finding new digs was complicated by the fact
that I had to break cover during the day. And at the beginning
of that last week in April I discovered that there were already
two ships berthed in the docks. One was a Canadian Pacific
'Empress' which was safe enough, but the other was a Cunard
cargo boat on its way to the Great Lakes. That sight forced me
uphill. My own duplicity in saying that I'd got a place near the
libraries meant that I also had to find somewhere out of range
of the boarders at Girard's – which drove me west. As I
zig-zagged, upward and westward, on and off buses, making
enquiries, I soon realised that the course I was pursuing might
as well be a graph which plotted the escalation of rents. Every
landlady I tried that first day was more expensive than Madame
Girard, even including her increase, which I was not yet paying.

When we were all gathered round the dinner table in the
evening and Jean-Pierre was plunging his alert, oily head into
conversations under the pretext of serving food, I prayed that
he would not mention to the others that I'd been out all day.
Fortunately, Gillespie seemed to be claiming all the attention.
It seemed that he'd spent the entire morning on the phone to
features editors in the UK, fixing the length and rate for articles
he persuaded them they had to have. That fascinated Jean-Pierre
– especially what the Scotsman was going to get paid. 'You just
describe what's right *here*?' he asked with sly incredulity. Making
money from what had always been under his nose was a con
that compelled his respect.

'An' what it *feels* like to be right here,' Gillespie added.

'It will feel like an explosion!' cried Emile enthusiastically. 'The great World Fair.'

'It's a pity that Otto will miss it,' I said.

Emile waved his hand to dismiss such an idea. 'No, no! He will not. I have promise I will go there for him. I will go there one day for me, one day for him – many times.'

The Scotsman demurred, 'That's no' the same thing, is it?'

'It is *better*! I will enjoy it for him better than he would enjoy it.'

We laughed and Gillespie nudged Paul who, keeping his eyes on his plate, nodded in the sage manner he had lately adopted. 'That is true. Whenever I am too tired to do anything – or afraid it will not be wonderful – I always send Emile. Then I know I have not wasted my time. Otto will not be disappointed.'

Emile beamed at this endorsement of his abilities but felt he should mention an unfair advantage. 'It is because I am young,' he confessed. 'People over twenty-five should not go anywhere.'

Still smiling, I took the appropriate moment to ask Gillespie, 'What age are you?'

'Twenty-seven, how?'

'It just goes to prove that Emile is wrong,' I said; but it proved instead that Otto had been right.

By Wednesday the Cunarder had moved on upstream towards Ontario and I had been forced considerably further downhill and east again. But apart from the fact that there was nothing under thirty dollars – and that was *without* meals – I became aware of something that should have been obvious from the start. In that quarter they did not want to take in Englishmen. Quite a few times I was told they could not offer me anything, even before I discovered that I couldn't afford it anyway. Many of the stairways were daubed with the Québec Libre motto. I began avoiding those marked houses but then ran into a few householders who were one-way bilingual. They listened to and understood my questions in English, but insisted on replying in Québécois – which I could not even begin to understand.

Apart from becoming depressed and angry, I became exhausted. Three days of climbing hills, climbing stairs and walking miles led to a sullen stupor at the dinner table. From this, with perverse relish, Gillespie tried to rouse me. He was getting on very well with the other boarders on the top floor and they, it seemed, had taken to him. From their laughter and chatter I gathered that they had reclaimed room five as their common room once again – just as it had been when Otto was there. I fervently wished that Otto was there now. He was the only person in the house to whom I'd told nothing but the truth and consequently the only person with whom I could have discussed my present situation.

'Are you goin' tae come, Bill?' Gillespie was asking me.

'What?'

'Get yer mind off the bloody Indians and listen to what we're sayin'.'

'What were you saying?'

The Scotsman made a gesture which invited Paul to be spokesman. Paul explained, 'We are arranging an outing, now that the main roads in the Laurentians are open again. We would go in my car on Sunday, and we wonder if you . . .'

Gillespie interrupted with hearty assurance, 'And we're willin' tae put up wi' an English interloper – as long as he minds his manners.'

The anger and implied insults of the day had more to do with my reaction than what Gillespie had actually said. It was with some difficulty that I kept my voice even. 'No, thank you, Paul. I don't think I'd want to go to the end of the street with such a loud-mouthed Scotch yobbo, much less drive up to the mountains. But if you get him there, do us all a favour and leave him there.' Getting to my feet I moved towards Gillespie who was between me and the hallway. He watched me every step of the way and did not move his head a fraction as I stopped at his shoulder to add, 'And I don't give a fuck what *you* think about manners, or anything else.'

I waited for his response. He looked up at me very steadily and said, 'Good night, Bill.'

Having nodded to the other attentive faces I marched off to

my room and slammed the door on all of them. The *Montreal Star* was already laid out on the desk and open at the Accommodation columns; a street map of the city covered my bed and once more I set to work. There was just one more day to find a room. For I would have to give a week's notice to Madame Girard on Friday, while she in turn would give the same notice for the rent increase. Moreover, it was understood that the tenants were technically obliged to vacate the premises at the end of the terms on which they had rented even though they intended to accept the new terms. In practice they just sat tight and paid up. In my case it was entirely possible that I'd come back one evening to find my belongings stacked at the street entrance. There was no protective shilly-shallying over the rights of the sitting tenant in Montreal. He hadn't any.

Thursday brought a fine bright morning and the burbling of a radio announcer that the temperature was already forty-seven Fahrenheit and might reach fifty by noon. He also kept saying that this was the first real day of spring. It did feel like it as I set out on my last chance search. And I had a plan. The idea occurred to me that the poor areas of the city would not be confined to those parts east of Mount Royal. The rates probably tailed away just as sharply on the other side as well. And there the English influence was stronger.

With frequent and bewildering changes of buses the long trek from one end of the island to the other seemed to take hours. But I began to feel confident and optimistic near the end of the journey as I noticed the increasingly run-down and industrial surroundings through which we were moving. I had not been in that area before, except briefly when I'd come ashore there.

Having decided that I could do without lunch I plunged straight into the door-knocking. After only three attempts I found the ideal place. It was not a boarding-house but just a room in a large flat occupied by a family. Mrs Delancy invited me in to see if I'd like it. She seemed rather vague about terms and, in many ways, reminded me of the delightful landlady I'd had when I was an apprentice. When I pinned her down to saying exactly what she wanted me to pay she hazarded, 'We were thinking, maybe, it would be about fifteen dollars a week.'

Astonishment produced a curious gurgle in my throat as I asked, 'And what would it be with half board?'

'What do you mean?' she asked, tilting her head like a worried bird.

'I mean food. How much would it be if I have my meals here?'

'Oh, of course you would have your meals here. The fifteen dollars is for the meals as well,' she said, smiling. 'All in,' she added, as though fearing she'd carelessly overestimated my intelligence.

'That's excellent. I'd like to move in at the end of next week, if it's convenient.'

'Whenever you like, Mr . . . er . . .'

'Thompson. That's a week on Saturday.'

'Right you are, Mr Thompson. We'll expect you then.'

So filled was I with relief and euphoria that I found myself in the street without being conscious of having come down the stairs from the flat. And now I was hungry and under no pressure whatever to deny myself lunch. The chief drain on my savings was about to be halved. There was a small cafeteria across the street and I headed for that.

Then it was as though I'd been thrown heavily on my back. For as soon as I sat down I saw Derek Pattison. And he saw me. I watched recognition, astonishment and uncertainty as to how he should proceed chase across his face. He started by smiling then moving quickly towards me. Probably I should have bolted for the door and given him the further dilemma of whether or not to pursue me, but I didn't. Quite incongruously, I smiled back. He said, 'Surely you haven't been sitting *here* for six months!'

'Hello, Derek.'

'You're a lot thinner,' he said, sitting down not opposite me but alongside on the bench, to block any sudden movement.

'I've been getting a lot of exercise.'

'I expect you know your father's been raising hell with the company.'

'No, but it doesn't surprise me. He's pretty liberal when it comes to attributing blame.'

Derek composed his face to suggest gravity. 'Of course, at first he thought you might be dead.'

'Now that I'm not, what is he blaming the company for?'

'Well, he's not sure yet, is he? I mean nobody was sure until now. I mean, when I . . .'

'When you tell them.'

His uncomfortable fidgeting bumped my elbow. 'Christ, Bill, I've got to tell them! That is, if you're not coming back with me.'

'But that's exactly what I plan to do,' I lied. 'That's why I'm here. I was just waiting to do that.' From his expression I could see that he didn't believe me. Yet there was nothing he could do until I proved that he shouldn't believe me. He glanced around the cafeteria looking for a 'phone and wondering if he would be justified in calling the police – even the dock police. I followed the direction of his eyes. Neither of us could see a 'phone. 'Awkward,' I said.

He intertwined his fingers and paid close attention to them as he stretched them backwards. 'It is embarrassing.' He looked towards the table he'd vacated and then at the bare table in front of me. 'You were just going to have something to eat, I suppose.'

I nodded. It was clear that the longer he kept me there the more likely it was that some more of our friends would arrive to aid the capture. I tapped his arm and pointed out, 'It's a self-service.'

'Oh! Sure!' He slid himself off the bench but kept a position between me and the door as I moved towards the frosted-glass screen which fronted the counter. I stood reading the large menu card displayed there until another customer came up then moved behind the screen at the same time as he did. But instead of moving along the counter I leapt towards the fire-exit on the back wall. The release-bar gave a deafening clatter but my self-appointed guard probably mistook that for kitchen noises. From the loading-bay on which I found myself I jumped to the courtyard and ran along an alley into the back garden of a ramshackle bungalow. I waited a few moments for signs of pursuit but there were none.

It was while I waited hidden in the garden – squelching in the ground made soft by the sudden thaw – that for the first time the thought came to me: what I was doing, and had been doing for six months, just was not worth the effort. Considering the results so far, the likely outcome was failure. What could possibly be gained by two or three months more lying, and hiding and loneliness? I jerked my head free of a wet branch and tried to visualise the consequences. Even if I decided to go back now, I couldn't do it instantly. I'd have to get back to Girard's first and make arrangements. I moved forward through the garden towards a side road on which I could see the tops of cabs passing. Although I did not have enough money to take a cab the whole way back to the east end, it would take me clear of the immediate area and on to a bus route.

When I was about to get into a cab I remembered Mrs Delancy. I told the driver, 'No, never mind,' and slammed the door. He swore at me and veered wildly into the stream of traffic. But there was no avoiding the fact that I had told Mrs Delancy I would take that room and she would be expecting me a week on Saturday. That was a week in which she could find another lodger who *would* be able to live there.

Since the street entrance to her flat was directly opposite the cafeteria from which I'd escaped it took me some time to reconnoitre and find a safe way to the back staircase. I told her I wouldn't be able to take the room after all and she immediately thought that I'd found somewhere cheaper. To convince her of the unlikelihood of that I advised her to increase her rent by at least ten dollars. She seemed doubtful but agreed to try it. 'By ten dollars,' I repeated, then realised that that was exactly the amount which had driven me to her in the first place.

By the time I got back to the far end of St Catherine East everyone had finished dinner and the dining-room was empty. When Madame Girard was alerted to my arrival she gathered herself to bestow one of her ultimate sighs before serving what had been saved.

When I'd eaten I went straight to my room and threw myself down on the bed. There was no doubt about it, the game was over. I had no money to stay where I was and I had nowhere else to go. There seemed to be no alternative but to give myself up. Stacked on the bedside table with their bindings coming adrift were the only witnesses in my defence. And, thinking of those counsellors of my apprenticeship I picked up the topmost book, not altogether unconsciously looking for a sign. And I found it; not by lighting upon a significant passage but merely by wanting to go on reading what was there. Whenever I opened one of those notebooks I always wanted to go on reading to the end. I did so now.

Throwing the book back on the pile I swung my feet to the floor, and decided that the end had not yet arrived for me and the freedom I'd been pursuing. Frank Fogel, my fellow apprentice in Greenock, would not have approved of that. He would have found another way and he would have taken it immediately. Thinking of Frank, I was reminded of Hugh Gillespie. The solution was obvious. Painful and humiliating too, of course, but obvious. I forced myself to my feet, moved steadily to the door, then tramped right upstairs to room five. My feet sounded very loud on the narrow wooden stairway which was lit only by a small electric bulb in the corridor at the top.

I tapped on the door which was ajar and Gillespie called, 'Come in!'

Upon opening the door wider I discovered that Emile, too, was in the room. They both stared at me with a kind of wary astonishment. 'Oh, I'm sorry. I didn't know you were here, Emile.'

'Emile is always here,' Gillespie grunted. 'All he's got in his room is an ice-box full o' ma beer and a bed.'

The Frenchman stood up. 'Would you like a beer?'

'No, thank you. I just wanted to talk to . . . Hugh . . . for a moment.'

This, apparently, was a very encouraging sign for Emile smiled broadly, 'About a private matter?'

I swallowed hard. 'Yes.'

'I will return!' Emile declaimed, holding his half-empty bottle above his head. 'There is a letter must be written to my father.' He went out and gently closed the door behind him.

'Sit down,' Gillespie said. I moved one of the camp stools nearer to his armchair at the window, over which the metallic grey venetian blinds were now in place. He made a gesture after the departed Emile. 'He's got me tae write his letters home.'

'I didn't know you spoke French.'

'A don't. Ma job is just tae provide the current letter-home-padding in English and he translates it and adds a few personal bits.'

'That's very kind of you.'

'No' in the least! A've had years o' practice writin' bloody letters home.' He finished off his Molson and placed the empty bottle under his chair. 'But that's no' what you want, is it?'

'No.'

'Didnae think so; for you never seem tae get any mail tae *answer.*'

I let that go without comment and my feeling of wretched uneasiness increased. Now that I was there I could not imagine myself asking what I'd come upstairs with the specific and carefully-steeled intention of asking. There seemed to be no way of leading painlessly into the subject. But I had reckoned without Gillespie's acuity; and his hitherto unsuspected regard for the integrity of other people – even if they were people he disliked. Yet the silence lengthened almost beyond recall before he spoke. That, he judged, was enough time for me to come to the point if I was ever going to.

'I've had quite a bit o' luck,' he said, easing himself further into the chair, 'wi' the UK papers. Quite a few commissions for regular features of on-the-spot Expo.'

'Good,' I said. 'It must be quite difficult selling work on the telephone.'

'It helps if they know ye.' Again the silence edged beyond the normal span of a pause. I was about to break it when he asked, 'Dae ye want a loan?'

I reddened with embarrassment. 'No. No, I . . . I'm afraid it's more presumptuous than that. I don't know if Jean-Pierre told you, but I hoped to get this room when Otto left.'

Gillespie shook his head. 'Didnae know that.'

'You see, the rent I pay for the room downstairs is really more than I can afford.'

'Ye want tae swap rooms?' He looked at me carefully. 'Or is it more presumptuous than that?'

I smiled weakly. 'Yes, it is. In fact I came to ask if you'd consider letting me share *this* room . . . with you.'

To my immense relief he considered only for a moment then replied with a kind of casualness that was positively graceful. 'A think that would work out fine,' he said.

'Of course, I haven't yet mentioned the idea to Madame Girard that is, Jean-Pierre.'

'A don't think ye should.'

'But I can scarcely move up here without . . .'

'No.' He brought himself upright in the chair. 'A mean, let *me* talk tae Jean-Pierre about it.'

'Why should you take that trouble?'

'Because there will be less trouble if A do.'

I immediately saw the truth in that. I'd noticed that young Girard was noticeably attentive and wary in his dealings with the Scotsman. 'I suppose you're right. How do you manage to charm that little creep?'

'It's no' charm,' Gillespie said. 'He's feart A might punch him in the face.'

I laughed, 'And would you?'

'Without a second thought.'

Of course there was more to Gillespie's willing acceptance of a room-mate than a humane wish to help somebody down on their luck. I knew he wanted to find out whatever it might be that I was hiding. And he would. Part of the relief I felt that Thursday evening was the obligation from then on to tell the truth. There would be no possibility and little point of either of us trying to conceal anything from the other. But it was not until later I realised Gillespie knew at the time he would soon need help in pursuing *his* secret mission in Montreal. Meanwhile, he did his best to dispel any awkwardness or embarrassment I might still be feeling.

'A hope ye realise,' he said, 'that ye might find it hard tae get much writin' done up here. Emile an' Paul an' Carlo treat it as open territory.'

'I did, too. When Otto had it.'

Oh, aye! That was before you . . . er . . . went intae purdah.' He rose quickly from the armchair, crossed to the wastepaper basket and dropped his empty bottle there before pivoting slowly on his heel to face me again. 'Maybe A should ask ye for references.'

'I have none.'

Gillespie nodded. 'The hell wi' references.' He made an elegant gesture, 'Even so, ye might as well try the armchair,' he said, and waited until I had settled myself in it before going on. 'When you frequented this room before . . .'

I smiled, '"Frequented". I haven't heard anyone say that for a long time.'

'It's a word in frequent use in Scotland.'

'Yes, I know. That's where I frequently heard it.'

Gillespie grinned, 'Oh, aye. The Greenock Apaches use it a lot. Anyway – when you used tae come up here before, were ye told aboot the woman next door?'

'No. You mean that door?' I pointed to the door between the beds which was defended by a steel bar.

Gillespie nodded. 'Her name's Yvette. She turns up the volume on her television very loud at certain times. Always channel ten.'

'She must be very fond of rock.'

'Naw. She's very fond o' cock. In fact she's a nympho. But all you'll hear is drum beats an' synthesisers. Very loud. Sometimes it's jist for half an hour or so, sometimes all night. Depends on what she's got in there – a solo fucker or a relay team.' He shrugged. 'Jist thought ye should know.'

'And how often does it happen?'

'Regular.' He moved to go out.

'Do you think Madame Girard knows about this?'

He pointed at the steel bar across the door. 'Why else d'ye think she put that up? Oh aye, she knows but she's likely gettin' a good rent.'

'You mean the woman in there is a prostitute?'

'A believe not. They say she jist does it for love, or tae cure her cough.' He turned again to go out. 'Now, A'd better go and see that wee ratbag Jean-Pierre. Ye want tae move up here on Saturday an' we share the rent – right?'

'Yes.'

'Okay. A'll tell 'im.'

I heard him go stumping down the stairs and Emile, reckoning that the private conversation must be over, returned. 'Hugh was telling me about channel ten,' I said.

Emile consulted his watch. 'It is too early!' He raised his head in an intent listening posture. 'No. I cannot hear it. Not even the coughing that comes before it.'

'I didn't know whether to believe him or not. About Yvette.'

'Oh, believe him! It is true.'

'Why did nobody tell *me* about this?'

'We do not think that you will be interested.'

'But I'm fascinated.'

'Ah,' Emile sighed, 'that is "interested" – at a distance.' He placed his palms prayerfully together and bowed towards the barred door. 'Madonna of Channel Ten, please grant us peace. Just a little piece.'

'Why do you call her, "Madonna"?'

Emile raised his eyes. 'Because she is always being ascended – into heaven by the sound of it.'

FOUR

The transfer from one room to another was accomplished without much difficulty. Jean-Pierre did whine a bit to me about the inconvenience but I consoled him with the thought that it would soon be snapped up by a rich American tourist. Madame Girard herself seemed to take the loss of a bird in the hand with more composure; aided no doubt by the additional barrage of joss-sticks she set smouldering that Saturday morning. It made lunch quite a heady affair.

After lunch Gillespie and I came to terms with the ground-rules for dual occupation. In such a sparsely furnished room there was no question of dividing the space. We just divided the number of drawers available for storage. I had the lower three in the plum-coloured tallboy behind the door. Gillespie had the drawer in the child's desk and I had the small cabinet which formed the bedside table. Since there was no wardrobe and Gillespie's hook on the back of the door would have buckled under any further weight I borrowed Paul's freestanding clothes-rack. He had a wardrobe but had preferred to hang his clothes in the open where the air could get at them. However, Jean-Pierre refused to let us move that wardrobe because it would mean repainting the wall behind it, so Paul nobly lent me his rack. We placed it in the corner of the room furthest from the window.

When everything that could be put away was put away I gave closer attention to my new accommodation. The walls were painted or distempered in pale green and decorated with no more than two large posters; one a copy of the bullring at Arles

and the other advertising cigars a good way after Lautrec. To
these Gillespie had added two shirt-pack cards one above the
other to make a long listing board on which he and Emile recorded
a week-by-week summary of the serious crimes reported in
greater Montreal. The sheet was lined off in columns so that an
accurate score could be kept. Scattered around the room were
the only other additions he had made. They were ashtrays.
There were half-a-dozen large glass ashtrays, deep green in
colour and shaped like halved turnips. He'd bought the lot very
cheaply at a fire-sale just along the block.

When I was distributing my own effects among the few
available locations Gillespie could not avoid seeing a large photograph of me and my parents seated in the garden at home.

'That your folks?'

'Yes.'

'What uniform is that ye're wearin'?'

'The Merchant Navy.'

'When was it taken?'

'A couple of years ago.'

There was a pause. He was waiting, I thought, to give me the
opportunity to change the subject or object to the questioning. I
did neither, so he went on. 'Ye've jist recently become a writer,
then?'

'I'm afraid I haven't become a writer yet.'

He looked closer at the photograph. 'Is that no' an engineer's
badge?'

'Yes.' I was relieved to re-establish at least some of the truth
in such a flat, uninvolved series of questions and answers.
'When that was taken I'd just completed my first trip as Second
Engineer on the *Lycomedes*.'

'Marine engineer,' said Gillespie, almost as a sigh. 'That
explains what might keep ye five years withoot a bath in
Greenock.'

I smiled and nodded, 'My apprenticeship.'

He raised the photograph again. 'Is that where this was
taken?'

'No, that was taken in Sussex.'

'What's the big house?'

'That's our house. I mean my parents' house.'

Gillespie whistled softly. 'The whole lot o' it?'

I nodded. 'That bench is in the garden.'

'Ye'll be tellin' me next it was the gardener took the picture!'
he scoffed.

My laugh disguised the fact that, if he'd asked, that was what
I'd have had to tell him. He showed less interest in my notebooks
as I stacked them on top of the bedside cabinet alongside one
of his enormous ashtrays. But certainly he understood that this
exposed position meant that the material was not private and
thus was open to his inspection whenever he felt any curiosity
about it. Of course privacy in that situation was a moral concept
rather than a defensible reality. There were no locks on any of
the drawers – or, at least, no locks that worked. Clearly this
did not bother my room-mate but initially it took a great effort
on my part to accept such laxness.

Gillespie and I were very formal with each other during this
settling-in period. And in the following few days, each of us was
keenly aware of the other's ability to provoke annoyance. My
own primary 'good resolution' was to make the effort to call him
Hugh. His, I think, was to try and overlook my accent if not
my giveaway cleanness. Very soon, though, he came to the
bargaining point that he'd had in mind when he agreed to share.
We were in the resting positions which became established as
normal. He sprawled in the armchair at the window and I sat up
on my bed with my back against the head-board. His bed was
between us.

'Bill, when Expo opens A'd like it fine if there was always
somebody in this room.'

'You or me, you mean?'

'Mainly, aye. But the other lads tae, if they'll agree.'

'Why? There's nothing worth stealing, is there?'

He pulled himself up into a more businesslike position. 'It's
no' that. Y'see A'm expectin' somebody.' He pointed to the
Montreal Star which lay folded on the desk. 'If ye look in that
paper ye'll see . . .'

'Yes. I've seen it. Your advertisement.'

His lips tightened and I chided myself inwardly for presumption. He took out his cigarettes and lit one before continuing, 'If anybody answers that advertisement, the paper will give them this address. But A cannae be here all the time.' He gave me an airy, speculative look. 'On the other hand, you seem tae prefer stayin' in.'

'That's true.'

He now gave great attention to getting ash which had not yet accumulated on his cigarette into the ashtray at his feet. 'So A thought, in exchange for living here – free – ye wouldnae mind . . .'

'Holding the fort?'

He nodded and I considered the offer. If he paid for my board as well as my bed then my stay in Montreal could be prolonged until October. 'Can you afford that?' I asked.

'A widnae have mentioned it if A couldnae afford it,' he retorted sharply. 'What A *can*nae afford is for the person tae come here and draw a blank.'

'All right.'

'Ye don't mind?'

'No. As you say, I'm in a great deal anyway. And I do want to help you locate . . . er . . . the person.'

He showed some irritation. 'His name is Sam Hanson.'

'I know.'

'Then how did ye no' *say* that?'

'Because I'm not sure if I'm supposed to know.'

He exhaled an impatient puff of smoke. 'Bill, it's hard for me tae get other people involved in this. Y'see, A know how ridiculous it might seem tae you or anybody else.' He paused to arm himself against the possibility of losing a new recruit. 'Jist try tae remember, it matters tae *me*. There's nothin' that matters *more* tae me. So, before ye start sniggerin' or gettin' off some sly wisecracks – think o' the damage. Okay?'

He did not expect an immediate reply. And that was fortunate.

Next day he pinned up a calendar wall-chart beside the crime tally. It soon became clear that both Emile and Paul were already well aware of Gillespie's quest and thoroughly approved of it. We all gathered round as the wall-chart was divided out as a duty roster. Basically, Hugh himself would do the mornings and

I would do the afternoons. The evenings were split up, bearing in mind Paul's courting schedule and Emile's various martial arts classes as well as Hugh's reluctance to stay in after dinner. Carlo was exempt because he was about to leave Girard's for a flat of his own.

But now that my help had been engaged in trying to find Sam and hold him, I felt free to ask how he had come to be lost. Of course, I chose the moment of my enquiry with care. More than once in those first few days our careful civility to each other was close to crumbling. At night, just after turning in was the least contentious time.

'Hugh, why didn't you keep in touch with Sam when he left Glasgow?'

'A wis abroad when he left.'

'Didn't he leave an address?'

'Sure. He left his address wi' his young brother.'

'Donny.'

'That's right.' I heard Hugh turn on his side so that he was facing me. 'It's hard for me tae realise, but at the time there was nae great urgency aboot gettin' in touch wi' Sam. That came later.'

'What happened then?'

'When A wrote tae Donny for the address, there wis nae answer. A thought he must have left as well. But he hadnae – no' then.'

I digested this information. It puzzled me that everything seemed so round-about. Until that moment I had not thought that Donny was of any importance and I could not imagine why he would wilfully ignore a letter from his brother's best friend. 'How did you get on with Donny?' I asked.

'Couldnae stick 'im!' Hugh declared flatly. 'Oh, he was all right at first. When A left school he wis jist a wean so he didnae matter.'

'How did he matter, later?'

'He grew up. Fast. He got intae bother an' Sam always had tae get him out o' it. Thievin', fights, then a whole raft o' wee hairies.'

'Prostitutes?'

He threw himself onto his back again, 'Naw! Prostitutes don't get pregnant. These were wee stupit lassies wi' dandruff on their shoes.'

I managed to disguise my involuntary laugh as a cough. 'How was Sam involved?'

'It was him had tae fight them aff wi' money or denial – the lassies themsels or their folks. Watchin' Donny got tae be a full-time job for 'im.'

'So he had less time for you.'

'He had less time for everythin'. That's what A wis trying tae put a stop tae.'

'How did you do that?'

'Why d'ye want tae know?'

Obviously my casual questioning had become too much like an interrogation. I tried to affect less interest. 'I just wondered what caused you to lose touch. If you hadn't, think of the trouble it would have saved.'

He was silent for a few moments, weighing the merits of this argument against a bad conscience. Then he asked, 'Hiv you got any brothers?'

'No. Nor sisters either.'

'Me neither. Though sisters widnae be much bother.'

Outside in the street the night freighter-trucks kept up their rhythmic passage with a sound like long breakers sweeping along a shore. As I inspected the high shadowy corners of the room, I wondered what Sam's parents had been doing while their younger son went to the dogs. But obviously any questions regarding them would far exceed my brief. Instead I asked, 'Did Donny follow Sam out to the States?'

'Within the year,' Hugh said. 'An' probably told Sam that A'd never written at all.' Hugh sighed. 'He was always very anxious tae get shot o' me, young Donny.'

I heard him turn onto his right side, to face the window; which meant he was going to sleep and would resent any thwarting of that intention. But I didn't sleep for quite a while as – quite pointlessly – I tried to reconstruct a situation it was difficult to understand, much less accept. For me the most salient point was that Hugh did not object to the young brother's thieving and fighting and raising pregnancies in girls with dandruff on their shoes. What he objected to was the distraction these activities caused.

When Expo was officially opened Hugh spent the whole of the first day there. He came back late and drunk. I woke as the door opened and the light from the landing wavered briefly across the room. Then I heard all the sounds that were familiar to me from my days as a junior engineer sharing a cabin aboard ship. There was the breathing pattern: a sharp inhaling and a slow exhaling; the moving feet that had the opposite sequence – a long step then the other foot brought quickly up to it; and then there was the inability to pick anything up at the first go. He didn't put on the light and eventually he got into bed. I turned over to resume my sleep and then I heard a sound with which I was quite *un*familiar – a man weeping.

I eased onto my back again and stared up at the ceiling listening to this new sound which was, somehow, both irritating and distressing. He started muttering, 'Moira! Moira! He wisnae there.' Then louder, 'The bastard wisnae there!' There was some more sobbing, but now more controlled. When he spoke again his voice was clearer for a moment. 'If the bastard gave a damn aboot me he wid have been there.' A few incoherent mumbles, then, 'But we *always* went the first day. He must remember that.' His breathing became more even and before long he fell asleep.

In the morning he was sharp and energetic as ever. 'Hope A didnae disturb ye last night.'

'No. You were very quiet, except for what you told Moira.'

'Moira!' He laughed. 'Was A talkin' tae Moira? That'll please her. Must let her know.'

'Where is she?'

'At home. Moira's ma wife.'

'I didn't know you had a wife.'

'Oh, *aye*! Been married for seven or eight years.' He got out of bed and padded to the armchair, over the back of which his trousers were folded and stretched to maintain their crease.

Again I noted that he was one of those men who look much bigger when they're stripped. He started pulling on his trousers. 'What was A tellin' Moira?'

'I think you were telling her that you couldn't find Sam at Expo yesterday.'

He stopped with his trousers incongruously at half-mast and gave me a long puzzled look. 'A see,' he said, resuming dressing. 'In that case she widnae be very pleased. She's sick tae death hearin' aboot Sam.'

That threw me momentarily. 'Does she know him?'

'Of course she knows 'im. He was best-man at the weddin'.'

He plucked his towel off the rail behind the door and headed for the bathroom.

This last sighting of Sam was much later than I'd assumed from the various snippets of information and recollection in Hugh's earlier conversations. From those I now knew that Hugh and Sam grew up together in one of the bleak new housing estates on the outskirts of Glasgow. They went to the same Catholic school and at first Hugh had been only a junior member of the gang, or 'team', of which Sam was the self-appointed but unchallenged leader. It was when they left school and the team was disbanded that the two became inseparable. Sam went to work in one of the shipyards of the upper Clyde and Hugh got a job in a local newspaper. It was then, when they were earning money, that they started going to World Fairs in European cities. Apparently the heady combination of being young, escaping from Glasgow, going abroad, being free agents and sharing the imaginative leaps and splendours of such exhibitions gave them both a feeling of invulnerability. As Hugh said, 'By Christ, we felt we were anointed!' And the feeling persisted. More; it took on the importance of obligation and covenant. The gut-felt obligation was to maintain the separate identity they could inhabit when they were away from home and together. The covenant was always, if it was humanly possible, to attend the World Fair.

Then Sam emigrated to Canada and from there planned to move down into the States. Hugh himself did a stint in London before moving out as a freelance in Europe. That they lost touch with each other – by Donny's intervention – was something which Hugh now angrily regretted. 'Since then A've had no luck whatsoever, and *nothing* goes right.'

'You seem to be doing not so bad,' I said.

'But it's no' *real*! Sam is the only person that knows the truth as A know it, an' is prepared tae say what it is. For him everything was real; no' always pleasant, mind you, but real as all get out. He saw me as I am and it didnae bother 'im.' He paused and smiled to acknowledge such fanciful idealism. 'That's what A miss. Now and then it's good tae be told ye're a bloody liar by somebody ye can trust.'

'And if he comes, what will you do?'

'Make sure A don't lose him again, that's the first thing. A'll know where he lives and where A can reach him if it's necessary. Apart fae that, we could get away somewhere.'

'Where?'

'What the hell does it matter, where? Peru!' Seeing my amazed look he laughed self-consciously and nodded, 'Aye! When we were boys we swore somehow we'd get tae Peru and re-sling that bridge at San Luis Rey. Exactly as it was.'

'I believe there is no *real* bridge of San Luis Rey.'

'Then there sure as hell should be. How are the buggers managin' withoot a bridge?'

'Why don't you go, yourself, and find out?'

'It's no' the same thing. We have tae be *needed* in Peru. Baith o' us.'

He'd proposed the jaunt to Peru when he was planning a more immediate strategy. That was a couple of days before the Expo opening and he was studying an enormous coloured photograph of the Expo site which he had just pinned on the wall above the child's desk. The two long islands lying abreast of each other in the St Lawrence were clearly laid out, as were the hundred or so individual pavilions. More important were the entrance points from the surface Expo Express and the Metro and the most likely route that Sam would take when he got there.

'You must have some idea where he would go first,' I said.

'Well – he widnae go tae the English, brackets British, pavilion, that's for sure. In fact the best bet might be the Trades

Centre, right over there at the harbour. They're havin' a big international engineering exhibition there.'

I shook my head, 'No, the best bet is that one.' I pointed to the huge geodesic dome of the American pavilion. 'That's the Piccadilly Circus of this exhibition. He may not go there first, but if he comes to Expo he will go there eventually. Everybody will.'

'True enough. But ye see, the monorail goes right *through* it, an' doesnae stop. There's that tae be considered, as well as the main entrance.'

We stared for a moment at the whole colourful panorama from the Cité du Havre to beyond the straddling spans of the Jacques Cartier bridge. And again I felt bound to say what I'd said on first hearing of the quest, 'It just is not possible. There will be millions of people, day and night for six months. How can one person be picked out, assuming that at some time he is there?'

'Bill, A *know*. A know, A know, A know all that. What I'm sayin' is – if there's a chance o' seein' him, where would be the *best* chance of seein' him. Right? Got it?' There was little wonder that he preferred discussing the operation with Emile who revelled in the 'Mission Impossible' aspect and was quite captivated by the whole idea.

On the day after the opening I stood staring at the site photograph as I waited for Hugh to return from the bathroom. He and Emile had spent the whole of that first day at Expo but, I suspected, Hugh had got drunk only after the Frenchman had returned to the digs. When he came into the room, his chest and upper arms glowing red from scrubbing, I said at once, 'They must have a public address system.' His expression brightened but, unfortunately, I felt it necessary to give an example, 'You know, like they have when little boys are lost in a big toy-shop.' The eager expression faded very suddenly and he brushed past me to put on his socks and shirt. As I went to take my turn in the bathroom I cursed myself for lack of thought. It was difficult always to bear in mind that this abrasive Scotsman was totally vulnerable in anything that concerned his 'witness'.

Although the duty roster was scrupulously marked up and adhered to, we were aware that the need for our guard duty depended entirely upon the effectiveness of a small entry in the Personal column of the *Montreal Star*. One morning at breakfast Emile outlined a bolder and much better plan. 'CJAD!' he exclaimed triumphantly.

'What?'

But Emile, who knew he had an ace, felt he could afford a step-by-step approach. He wedged the last of a jam-filled roll into his mouth and got it into manageable shape before continuing. 'This moment, the only real way you have to find Sam is the announce in the newspaper.'

'Advertisement,' Hugh corrected, nodding.

'And it is a very small announce. Also, who can say that every visitor from the States will buy the *Montreal Star*? And if he does, what reason will he have to look in the Personal column in a foreign city?'

'You've got a better idea?'

'Yes. CJAD is a radio station. Every evening Paul Reid has a long programme. He plays music, but people call him on the telephone just to talk. It is very pleasant.'

'In English?'

'Of course, in English! So – you must tell him about this crazy search. He would like the idea and he will talk about it on the radio.'

'Yeah!' Hugh saw at once that this was a scheme that would work. 'And it would sell Expo as well. They must be advertisin' on every station anyway. What dae you think, Bill?'

'Sounds very appealing.'

But their attention was distracted. The dining-room window overlooked the rear of the building and the exterior back staircase ran diagonally past it. Hugh and Emile looked out as a frail woman descended the staircase. She had dark hair piled high over her pale forehead. Following close behind her a young man of Latin appearance slapped the wood handrail at every step. When they'd descended out of sight Hugh and Emile moved their heads in unison to face each other, smile, then give one deep nod.

'Who was that?' I asked.

'That was Yvette.'

'Oh! How do you know?'

'Because A made it ma business tae find out.'

We were about to rise from the table when Jean-Pierre came bustling out of the kitchen clutching a sheaf of papers. 'One minute, guys, *if* you don't mind.' His voice rasped a little and he stood at the top of the table with his back very straight and his chin tucked well in. Clearly we were about to be treated to an early rehearsal of a new role. 'Thing is, we gotta fill in some forms. Why's that? Because the city wants records kept. Okay?' He threw the papers down on the table rather like an intelligence officer about to deal with a suspicious dossier. Then he dragged a chair into position by hooking his toe around one of its legs. He sat down with a sigh. 'I got the others before they went to work this morning, so now it's your turn.'

Already I was uneasy. 'What records does the city want? And why?'

'Well, Bill, you know we are now listed as guest-house accommodation for Expo. Right?'

'Guest house, b'god,' muttered Hugh, not entirely under his breath.

The youth rode over the interruption. 'Which means keeping tabs on the tourists and visitors, for statistics and all that crap, right?'

'Right,' agreed Emile, getting caught up in the performance.

Jean-Pierre bent his head to shuffle the papers in case there was a spontaneous burst of applause which it would be churlish to speak through.

'And what do they want to know?' I asked.

'Aw, simple. Very simple. They want to know names and home addresses of all residents. And name with address for next of kin.'

Hugh gave a shout of laughter. 'Huh! Next of kin? How many deaths dae they expect at your guest house?'

I was glad Hugh raised the first objection to that because I was perfectly sure the city required no such information. I was equally sure that it was information which Jean-Pierre intended to use for his own purposes. 'Yes. Why do they want to know that?'

Jean-Pierre gave a weary shrug worthy of his mother and in less time than it took to complete the gesture invented the first plausible reason that occurred to him. 'Suppose somebody gets sick. How they to know who pays for a doctor – even hospital, maybe?'

'Ye mean *after* they've been through his wallet?' Hugh wondered. 'Listen, son, A've lived in hotels all over the world and never once been asked for ma next of kin.'

'I gotta get the information they want,' Jean-Pierre stolidly insisted. 'If I don't fill the forms right, they send round a guy to check the passports and . . .' he glanced pointedly at Emile '. . . work permits.'

There was a prickly silence. He knew he had us because we knew that Emile had no such permit. Nor did I. In fact, even my passport was being held by others and I had much stronger reasons than Emile for avoiding any snooping by officials. For a moment I entertained the notion of giving a false name and address. But that would cause more trouble later, if detected. And there was little doubt that it would be. Young Girard had eagerly at his disposal the resources of an Immigration Department already in high gear to trap draft dodgers from the United States, not to mention the strict quota in force for United Kingdom citizens. Jean-Pierre passed down blank slips of paper for us to write the information. 'The forms are in French,' he explained. 'You can leave me to fill them in.'

Setting down the names and addresses, I was aware that Hugh was watching me very closely and with some concern. Obviously I wasn't managing to conceal my fear and apprehension.

He asked our interrogator, 'What if ye don't know the address o' yer next of kin?'

Jean-Pierre could see nothing wrong with the question, though he had a little trouble with the answer. 'Write, "return to sender" . . . No. Put "address unknown."'

Hugh grinned as he complied with that then, in an effort to cheer me up, passed his slip over to me. He'd written, 'Next of Kin – Sam Hanson; address unknown.'

'You know best,' I said.

FIVE

Gradually, I began to understand Hugh Gillespie and his challenging manner which initially I'd found so irritating. It arose from his always having been the junior partner in his relationships and having to assert himself to prove equal. When it was established that I was perfectly willing to allow him to be more than equal, much of the challenge evaporated, though the abrasive directness remained. His treatment of Emile and Paul was always affectionate and easy because, I reasoned, they were younger than Hugh. They were also very amiable persons. Emile in particular suited him well – except when they played chess together. The Frenchman was a fairly good player and could beat all of us except Hugh – who was a very bad player. This was because the anarchic Scotsman insisted on attacking with the King. It drove Emile wild because there was nothing in all the instruction or example he'd ever come across which offered a counter to such an insane ploy.

Emile complained to me, 'At chess he is crazy. What he should defend he ever advances. The castles, the knights, the bishops he uses like pawns and all are sacrifice. The queen he throws away. What way is that to play?'

'A'm tryin' tae beat the system,' Hugh informed him.

'With a better player than me you could only do it once.'

'Wi' a better player than you A'd only *need* tae do it once.'

At first I treated this gambit as a minor idiosyncrasy but it proved to be more than that because Hugh applied the same technique to many other aspects of his life. On a later occasion he told me, 'The secret is; never try to win the game – try tae beat the rules!' It was his method of dealing with authority, learned as a boy whose parents were the natural targets and victims of a legion of petty officials in the MSS, the Council, the School Board, the public utilities, hire purchase collectors and debt chasers. The Rules were all in their favour. The Rules had been made wholly for their convenience. The only chink in their armour was what they thought a strength – the Rules were inflexible. So when Authority came beating on the door, demanding entry, you let them in because you could not keep them out, but you held them to whatever rule they were enforcing while you attacked with the King.

'How could that be done?' I asked.

'By goin' over the score right away.'

'But how?'

Hugh settled himself to the exposition. 'Well, ye see maist o' the heavies we had tae deal wi' wanted money. They wanted money that ma faither or ma mother owed them. Take hire purchase – a three-piece suite. Ye default on that a few times and they send a bully-boy tae yer door, always at tea-time tae make sure ye'll be in. He wants the arrears cleared up or the firm'll take back the furniture. So ye jist shove it right at 'im! Ye insist he takes the three-piece suite that very minute. Ye shove it oot ontae the street so that he's got full possession o' it an' ye shut the door.' Hugh smiled and referred the recalled moment to his general thesis. 'Which means that ye've done tae him what he only *threatened* somebody else might do tae you.' He picked up on the next move. 'Now! The man's oot there on the street wi' the furniture an' he's *lost*. The shops are shut, his office is shut, and he hisnae the faintest idea how tae cope.' Hugh slapped the arm of the chair. 'So he leaves it! He jist walks away fae it! He abandons what you've made his firm's property. An' there are plenty of witnesses that he had possession. When he's well away ye jist open the door and say "My goodness! Look whi' somebody's thrown oot" – and ye take it in.'

'And does that work?' I asked.

'It works if ye dae it the very first time he comes. But then ye never hiv tae dae it again wi' the same firm. An' it works because their threat is tae take the furniture – but the furniture is the *last* thing they want.'

'Yes. I see that. But it's difficult to imagine how you can make that work with other threats.'

'Exactly the same way. Ye threaten tae carry them out – yoursel'. Claim arrest! Oh, many's the time A've run for the polis tae arrest ma old man. But by the time we got back whoever was threatenin' the arrest was gone. If ye call their bluff they cannae cope. The thing is tae dae it right there and then. It's the suddenness o' gettin' tae the end o' the line, when they've hardly started, that shakes them.'

I nodded, for I could see that attacking with the King had a great deal to commend it if all you had in mind was survival. The King may be defeated but he never leaves the field.

'But what did your neighbours think of all this?'

Hugh laughed. 'Bill, worryin' aboot the neighbours wis a luxury we could never afford.'

Not long after Jean-Pierre had collected our registration details he appeared at breakfast with a large and ornate registration book.

'Are ye gonnae put that on a wee table in the lobby?' Hugh asked.

'Nope. I'll keep it in my room. But we want you guys to sign your names at the dates you came here or under "Resident at January first".'

The book was passed around and we signed as he asked. There was also a space to declare 'Occupation' and I entered 'Writer'. That, as far as Jean-Pierre knew, was what I was and confirming the lie would, perhaps, edge the hope nearer to reality. But what was much more worrying than the book was the fact that the information we'd previously given had been used. Madame Girard's was now on the official list of guest houses and therefore on the list of places which would have quiet visits from various investigators whether they were looking for American draft-dodgers, illegal immigrants or criminals. I stared gloomily at the table top. After a moment I became aware that Hugh was watching me, and this time, I knew, he wouldn't be brushed off. When we got back to room five he immediately demanded, 'Well? What's botherin' ye?'

'You know that I used to be a marine engineer.'

'Aye. But that's aboot all A know.' In his voice there was more than a suggestion that whereas our sharing of the room had been fair, the sharing of information had been unequal. He'd proved himself willing enough to provide me with full and candid revelations but had received very little in return. As he moved away from the door towards the armchair Emile came in to join us. Hugh looked at me anxiously.

I shrugged. 'It's all right.'

'What is all right?' the Frenchman asked.

'It's all right if you know why I'm hiding here.'

'Ah! This is a matter of great interest to me.' He settled himself in a mock-judicial manner on a camp stool which was too low to confer much dignity. 'Also, why should it be that when the ice started to melt – you froze?'

Hugh twisted impatiently in the armchair. 'Emile, none o' yer nonsense. This is a serious business.'

I protested, 'No! He's quite right. When the ice melted the seaway was open to shipping. That meant the crews and agents of those ships would start moving around these parts. That's why I had to stay out of sight.'

'These people are looking for you?' Emile asked.

'Why?' Hugh wanted to know.

'Because I jumped ship. Last October when the *Lycomedes* was going downriver and heading for the Atlantic, I went over the side.'

There was a long silence which, eventually, Hugh breached. 'An' yer ship'll be comin' back?'

'It's already been back. I ran into one of the engineer officers not long ago. At this moment the *Lycomedes* is somewhere on the Great Lakes.'

Emile's eyes were wide with astonishment. 'You swam ashore in October?'

I laughed. 'No. The ship was going through the locks at Lachine.'

'So it couldnae well turn back!'

'Or wait. And of course that was the last trip before the winter set in and the seaway was closed.'

Emile asked, 'Why would you do such a thing?'

'I was . . . under some pressure that I couldn't really deal with. If I'd gone back to the UK on that trip the situation would have got even worse.'

'This must have been very serious that you should run away.' Emile's tone suggested that a pillar of the establishment had revealed a gaping crack.

'It was very serious to me. It still is.' But immediately I realised that I was placing quite the wrong emphasis on the affair. To lift the gathering pall I added, 'Besides, I wanted to try my hand at writing a novel.'

'This bloke ye ran intae – will he report ye?'

'Certainly.'

Hugh grinned and guessed, 'Ye were no' very popular on the ship.'

'Right. And less popular now.'

'If they find you, what will they do? Emile asked.

'Well, they won't shoot me.'

'When dae ye think yer ship'll be back this far?'

'I don't know. She may be on a round-trip or she may be trading between ports on the lakes. But since I met Pattison they certainly know I'm here. And all the authorities will know as well. That's why I wasn't very keen on Jean-Pierre's census.'

'That wis a lot o' nonsense!' Hugh said.

'Yes. But I can't ignore it.'

'You can grow a beard,' Emile suggested.

'No good. My beard doesn't match my hair. I tried it once aboard ship and it looked like red wool.'

'But you could have a red wig!' As always, the young Frenchman's attention had moved quickly from the hard facts of the matter to its more fanciful aspects.

Nor was Hugh much concerned with the consequences of my action. What amazed him was that I should have done it at all. He shook his head wonderingly and smiled, 'There's hope for ye yet, Bill. A deserter, b'God!'

During the first few weeks I spent in room five the end of winter lurched wildly into the middle of summer. The whole of spring seemed to happen overnight. Despite the increasing heat, Hugh worked at a furious pace. And though for a time he tried *not* to interfere with my desultory pecking at the typewriter, I could see he thought I was just plain lazy. He found it difficult to believe that anyone given the advantages that I'd been given could – without some ulterior motive – make such a hash of it. He sympathised, of course, with my avowed search for freedom but despaired that I had accomplished so little in seven clear months of trying to be a writer.

And I started learning immediately. To start with, he showed me the perfect position for typing. He placed the machine squarely on the foot of the bed and sat on a chair, legs apart, facing it. It was a method which he'd found to be the only true method by years of experience in working from hotel rooms. There is no doubt that it reduces the *noise* of typing considerably, and the vacant portions of the bed at either side of the machine are available for draft and notes respectively. Also, since the main light fitting is usually in the centre of the room, the illumination falls ideally on the page from above and behind the operator. 'But the main thing is,' Hugh said, 'that it's the right height.' He grew quite heated on the subject. 'It sickens me, y'know, when ye see photographs o' them authors in their tweed jaickets sittin' at their typewriters on desks – and the desks are *always* too bloody high! Nae wonder the buggers need secretaries. Ye cannae type a fair copy wi' yer elbows oot like wings; an' if ye could, ye couldnae dae it for mair than twenty minutes withoot cramp.' He snorted contemptuously. 'Naw, naw. You show me a writer wi' his machine on the end o' the bed an' A'll show ye a pro. And no matter where ye travel – tae rooms wi' ramshackle desks or rickety tables at every level – the bed is always strong enough tae take the weight o' the machine, and always the same height off the floor.'

We developed a routine in which he typed during most of the morning and I typed during the afternoon when he was out. Sometimes we overlapped after dinner, when there would be a typewriter going at the end of each bed. Emile, who had the adjoining room, coped with this barrage very well. He came in and watched us for, as he explained, a noise is less annoying when you can see what's *making* the noise. One evening about the middle of May he supervised for only a few minutes before announcing, 'It is Otto's turn to go to Expo, and he wants you to come along, Bill. He thinks it is ridiculous you have not yet been there.'

'So dae A!' Hugh growled, slamming the carriage return.

'I'm a man on the run,' I reminded them.

'But what running can you do sitting here?' Emile demanded. 'What is the fun of being hunted if you don't give the hunters a chance?'

Hugh completed a paragraph and straightened his back. 'That's true. Ye've got tae gie them a square go, Bill.' He pointed to the site photograph, 'And ye really must see that place. It's magic!'

'Paul will take us in his car,' Emile said, moving to the door. 'I will tell him now.'

'Then who'll stand duty?' I asked.

'This once, jist forget the roster. He'll no' pick this wan night fae so many.'

'Wait a minute! You've no idea what I'm risking.'

'Ye're riskin' damn all,' Hugh asserted, waving Emile to complete his errand. 'If A cannae find Sam there, how's anybody gonnae find you?'

I had to admit the justice of that. I'd often enough told Hugh that he hadn't a hope of success at Expo. And now, for the first time, it occurred to me that my situation was the exact opposite of his. My future and his past could be equally elusive. I smiled. 'It would be a shame to spend all this time in Montreal and not see Expo at least once.'

'That's the spirit! Try everything once. An' don't worry – if somebody tries tae nail ye, we'll swear blind ye're somebody else.'

'Who?'

'Who would ye like tae be?'

'Sam?' I suggested.

'Ye'd have tae go some.' He shook his head. 'No. From what

I've heard you'd be better as Otto.' At that moment Emile returned. Hugh told him, 'Bill's gonnae be Otto.'

'Oh, good! Then I can go as myself again.' He looked down at his clothes. 'I'd better change his shirt. Also, his underwear.'

Hugh grabbed his arm to prevent any further time-wasting diversions and we waited for Paul to emerge from the room at the end of the corridor. As we set off in the car I had the feeling that we were wrong to leave the top floor unmanned. This might well be the evening when Sam knocked on the door of room five. And we would never know if he had called.

'"Is there anybody there? said the Traveller,"' I quoted to Hugh and repeated my misgivings.

'He'll no' come on a horse,' the Scotsman reassured me, and we sped away in the Oldsmobile through a canyon of tawdry neon towards wonderland.

From the open top deck of the French pavilion and looking around us, we thought that there could be no scene in the world more ravishingly beautiful than Expo '67 at night. The national and provincial pavilions covered the two islands, joined by graceful bridges and fretted with canals, still pools and soaring fountains. The shapes and colours and textures of the pavilions caught in glowing light or silhouetted against the dark river contrived, for all their variety and individual design, to give the impression of a single enchanted dream-world afloat in the warm air. Of course, the others had seen it before but I was aware from the way they glanced at me that my seeing it increased their pleasure at the sight. And everywhere we looked there were smiling people. They strolled along the river paths or on the raised walkways; they were drawn in tiny coaches along the high, weaving monorail. In the distance those illuminated coaches seemed no more substantial than gleaming beads of water sliding along a spider's web. The night-scented flowers, stirred only by the surface movement of the river, gave up a fragrance which was hard to define. Indefinable, too, was the faint music heard in so large a space under the open sky. I gazed steadily over the whole magical landscape as though if I even blinked it might vanish. I murmured to Hugh, 'How could men make something as beautiful as this?'

'It's a great place tae be,' he said.

'How does it compare with the others you've been at?'

'Nae comparison.'

'And that's what you'll say at the next one.'

He shook his head vehemently. 'Naw. A'll no' be goin' tae any more. Nobody, *ever*, is gonnae do it better than this.'

The four of us stood in line, arms resting on the topmost rail and elbows touching. Paul who was handsome, methodical and businesslike; Emile, a young and inexperienced genie who'd just discovered how to get out of the bottle and was bent on mischief; myself, who did not deserve to be with them at all; and Hugh, square-faced and compact, making the most of his last chance. In some ways we knew all that needed to be known about each other and, in the main, were pleased by what we knew. Certainly we were glad to be there that evening together, standing on the high pavilion, immune from the past and the future. I hoped I would remember the moment; the persons we were then, how it looked, how it felt. Even how it smelt, for mixed with the scent of flowers there was the smell of creosote rising from the rough timbers which formed the deck on which we stood. The words that Hugh had used earlier came back to me. Christ! we felt as though we were anointed. Now I appreciated what it meant to feel invulnerable and set apart. And I began to realise the nature and strength of the obsession which Hugh sustained against all odds. 'I think you will find it,' I told him.

'Him, ye mean?'

'If he still has it, you may find him as well.'

Hugh nodded – sure that he would.

SIX

The fact that I'd been taken into the protective custody of the top-floor fraternity enabled me to get out and around with them. Tennis was the favourite, though the fact that there were only three of us at any one time precluded effective doubles play. This suited Hugh, who had never played tennis before and was now determined to make up for all the years during which he'd never realised it could be such a hard aggressive game. He certainly didn't want to be hampered by a feckless partner.

We spent quite a number of early summer evenings at Parc Maisonneuve which was the site of golf courses and botanic gardens as well as public tennis courts at which all the gear could be hired. It was unlikely that these amenities high on the hill would attract the crews or agents of ships which passed far below. But while we diverted ourselves there, a meeting that was to have significant effect upon Hugh Gillespie and me was taking shape at the Cité du Havre. In the Trade Centre which was part of Expo, an international group of engineers gathered at a four-day State of the Art conference and seminar. To represent Colin Thompson Partners of London came Mr Colin Thompson himself. But the largest contingent was made up of engineers from various companies in the United States. Among these was Mr Sam Hanson.

In the normal course of such conferences it would have been unlikely that Colin Thompson and Sam Hanson would meet in any but the most superficial manner. One was a member of the platform party and the other – though highly regarded by his

employers as an up-and-coming young manager – was a face in
the body of the hall. However, in one of the papers he delivered,
Mr Thompson alluded – as he was fond of doing – to a critical
solution at the Clydeside shipyard where he had started his
training. When questions were invited Mr Hanson stood up to
make a pertinent point that the same solution was being applied
more than thirty years later at that same shipyard where he too
had served his time. Mr Thompson and the assembled engineers
laughed appreciatively.

Later, in the bar, Mr Thompson good-naturedly pursued the
argument with the young Scots expatriate. They got on well
together. Thompson discovered that young Hanson had a very
sharp mind which was capable of assessing just how much of
modern innovation was progress and how much merely a hard
sell of a profitable product. Hanson, for his part, was flattered
to have gained the attention of so distinguished an engineer,
whose personal intervention had saved huge enterprises from
waste and loss. This middle-aged, plump and austere man was,
he knew, worth every dollar of the very large fees he and his
partners were paid by companies who vied for his services. In
the bar that evening Mr Hanson and Mr Thompson agreed that,
man or machine, the important thing was the ability to deliver
exactly what was promised.

At about the time when an international group of engineers
gathered to discuss the state of their art, an international group
of boarders had gathered in room five and begun discussing the
state of the city. We had just had dinner and that, combined
with the sticky heat of the evening, produced a rallentando effect
upon our conversation.

While Paul considered his next chess move, Emile picked up
the evening paper. He leafed through it and then remarked,
'That makes seven.'

'Seven what?' asked Hugh, without looking up from the letter
he was typing to his wife.

'Seven fires,' said Emile. 'Three murders and two explosions.'

I put down my book on my outstretched legs. I was propped

against the wall while resting on my bed. I tried to recall the score. 'That's better than last week, isn't it?'

Emile got up to check on the list that was pinned to the wall by the window. 'Only for the fires,' he reported. 'Last week we have only three fires, it is true, but we have a "multiple killing" as well as a regular murder; and an explosion, of course.'

'It is the heat,' Paul murmured from the armchair – idly staring at, but not concentrating on, the chess board he was supporting on his knees.

'Rubbish!' I told them. 'It's what comes of having all you Catholics together.'

'What?'

I explained, 'In Catholic countries the people kill each other. In Protestant countries they kill themselves.'

'There are many suicides in Glasgow?' asked Emile.

'Glasgow is half-Catholic,' I parried. 'Or thinks it is.'

'Edinburgh, then?'

'Edinburgh is a special case. The Reformation is still going on.'

'How about explosions?' Emile challenged me.

Hugh inserted a sheet of Tipp-Ex under the typewriter guard and struck a key. 'Very few, but that's because the English wulnae gie us any dynamite.'

'I should think not! Look what happened the last time we gave you some.'

Hugh grinned. 'Darnley had it comin' tae him, in my opinion.'

'But what a pity he waited until it arrived.'

'True! Arson would've been less obvious.'

Emile asked, 'What is "assen"?'

'Making fires – *specially*,' his chess opponent informed him. 'For insurance, and so.'

'Oh, we have some o' they fires in Glasgow.'

'Huh!' Emile grunted. 'In Montreal we have no *other* kind. Likewise, explosions.'

'Now, now, be fair,' Hugh chided. 'Explosions cost too much to be wasted on an insurance claim. But they *are* cheaper than demolition costs – and, of course, if ye can pack a few enemies in as well, that's all tae the good.'

Emile moved away from the tally sheet and sprawled once again on the floor at Paul's feet. He tried *willing* Paul to make a move – any move – while Hugh's typewriter clacked busily into the silence. He turned his attention there instead. 'Maybe when you have finish that one you will do a letter for me.'

'To France?'

'Yes.'

'Is yer faither any better?'

'No. He is still sick.'

'Does he like ma letters?'

'I do not tell him they are your letters. Anyway, the translation is much better.'

'Sure. But does he think *your* letters hiv improved?'

'He notices they are longer, now.'

'An' whit's yer mother say?'

Emile turned his attention again to chess and there was a pause before he mumbled, 'She does not read them.'

'Efter a' the trouble A take tae . . .'

Paul suddenly made a move, but as he did so he glanced quickly at Hugh and shook his head warningly. I was placed above them and intercepted the look. For the briefest moment, while Emile had legitimate reason to be preoccupied, the three of us acknowledged that we'd run into yet another of those delicate folds which ought not to be unfolded. It was astonishing how little we knew of each other's families; and sad how little it mattered. I remembered Otto warning me that Montreal was a young man's town – a stopping place to the next stopping place. 'For aliens,' he'd told me, 'Montreal is a big transit-camp.' And now that it was summer, the truth of this became apparent. One could see the 'aliens' walking the streets, impatiently, killing time; waiting for a message which would tell them they could move on. In such a situation there was no virtue in having parents. All you stood for, you stood up in. And you were assessed only on what you were at the moment you were assessed. I would learn nothing more about Emile's mother.

'Are you lot going out tonight?' I asked.

'Hélène is waiting for me at Dorval,' said Paul, 'and I will drive to her as soon as I feel strong enough.'

'I will go instead, if you like,' Emile offered. 'It will be a big change for Hélène.'

'As a pencil is a change from a broomhandle,' Paul confirmed amiably.

'Hugh? You going out?'

He resumed typing. 'Soon as A finish this, A'm away. If we go later than last night a' the cool places'll be crowded.'

Emile jumped his knight over a high invisible fence. 'We could go to a movie. Or take a walk round the Place Ville-Marie.'

'Movie as a last resort, but Place Ville-Marie gi'es me the creeps. Last time A went there A was accosted five times within the hour.'

Paul smiled. 'The women, you mean?'

'Three women and two men.'

Emile was interested. He rolled over on his stomach facing Hugh. 'What do the men say?' he asked. 'I know what the women say, but what do the men say? They do not say it to me.'

I raised my eyebrows. 'I wonder why not?'

Hugh unglued his back from the uncomfortable chair and thought for a moment. 'The men say, "Have you got a light?" or, "Do you know where the gents is?" or, "Isn't this a lonely place?"'

'Ah!' Emile was embarrassed and let his forehead bump gently on the floor. 'They have said *these* things to me. But I thought they *meant* these things!' He twisted away from our mocking smiles. 'Those crazy guys! How can they make any money if they ask such stupid questions?'

I stretched to turn on the radio which was on Hugh's side of the bedside cabinet. It was permanently tuned to CJAD 800 but I was too early for the Paul Reid show and turned it off again. The item would be broadcast, though. The station had made Hugh's one-in-a-million search their own and, twice a week, Paul Reid asked Sam Hanson to call *him*. Hugh was delighted about that, but less happy at the choice of music which introduced the item. It was a snatch of bagpipes playing 'Scotland the Brave'. Hugh had groaned, 'What the hell dae they think we are, bloody Teuchters?'

Emile rolled across the linoleum and broke surface at Paul's knees. 'Okay. Make a move. I am ready.'

Paul yawned and rolled his head to relax his neck muscles. 'I concede.'

'What!'

'I say you win.'

Emile was outraged. 'Say *nothing*! Move and *see* me win!'

At that point all hell broke loose around us. From the street came a series of ragged explosions which could not be more than a block away and next door Yvette turned up channel ten to a sudden fierce volume. Paul leapt to his feet catching Emile across the brow with the edge of the chess board and scattering the pieces on the floor. I was dazed by the sudden onslaught of noise but whereas Emile, Paul and I made for the window – Hugh made for the door. We heard him leaping downstairs two at a time. West of us and nearer the river a squat pile of dust and smoke was trying to rise into the still, humid air. For a few minutes Yvette had it all her own way but soon was eclipsed by a symphony of sirens and bells. Converging from all quarters were police cars, fire tenders, ambulances and hopeful 'wrecker-brakes'. They careered out of sight down a side street and one by one their sirens died in parox- ysms of fearful moaning. The barrel-shaped pall of smoke, denied altitude, started sliding sideways towards the river. Gradually the bustle of activity in the street subsided and we withdrew from the window. Emile went at once to the score card and added another hit on the week's tally, Paul started tidying his appearance to meet the patient Hélène and all of us became aware of the hectic activity on channel ten.

'Oh, Yvette!' wailed Emile. 'Let me be next.'

'You are no good for her,' said Paul, combing his glossy black hair. 'You only know one way to do it.'

'That is because I have only one thing to do it *with*!' the young Frenchman protested, indicating where the sole implement could be found. He wandered over to read the page which was still in the typewriter.

'I don't think you should read Hugh's letter,' I said.

'Why not? He writes mine.' He resumed his examination. 'It is to a girl called Moira.'

'Perhaps it is a love letter,' Paul said.

'No. There is no love in it. He is writing most about himself – and us.'

'Moira is Hugh's wife,' I said, and wondered why he hadn't told them.

Emile was immediately shamed. He drew back then turned abruptly away but I could see the back of his neck flush red. All of us were relieved to be able to turn our attention to a fresh burst of activity in the apartment next door. Even channel ten could not wholly cover or disguise the nature and rhythm of what was being done.

'That reminds me,' said Paul suavely, 'of something I should be doing. I think I will now drive very fast to Dorval.'

'You mean, drive hard.'

'No. That is what happens when I *get* to Dorval,' Paul said. And he went.

Since it seemed wrong to try and interrupt someone else's intercourse, Emile and I remained silent until events next door reached a calmer level and the television was switched off. Then it was Emile who resumed in a troubled voice, 'You will understand, I did not know Hugh is married. I think it is only a girl-friend he writes to.'

'Yes, I understand.'

'But why would he not tell me this important new?' He glanced at me. 'Why are you smiling?'

What I was smiling at was his habit of referring to a single item of news as a 'new', but in his present serious mood it would have been tactless to correct that. 'I think he doesn't want to mention anything that makes him seem settled or stodgy,' I said.

'Stodgy? What is that?'

'Well, serious and quiet and responsible.'

'Like you, this is. That Hugh does not want to be. Eh?'

I laughed and nodded. 'You can certainly take it that Hugh doesn't want to be like me.'

'But you are not married so how can that make a difference?' Emile asked.

'It seems to make a difference to him. Or, at least, in the picture he holds of himself.'

To my relief Emile did understand that very well. It was only material things that he had trouble with. 'Ah, yes,' he nodded, smiling. 'That will be why he acts so young and goes everywhere with us. I must say, Hugh makes it easy to see him as he really is.'

'I would have thought a wife was real enough,' I observed with more edge than I'd intended.

Emile responded to the tone of my voice more than the words. '*You* could have a wife if you wanted one, I suppose. In fact . . .' But then we heard footsteps on the stair and Hugh breezed into the room. Emile at once confessed, 'I have read your letter.'

Hugh threw himself on his bed. 'So?'

'So, what was the scene of devastation like?' I asked.

'What?'

'The explosion! You ran off to do an on-the-spot report.'

'Did A hell! Ye can see explosions any night o' the week around here. But Yvette, on the other hand, runs a pretty tight schedule.'

'Yvette?' As I said the word I was aware of rather goggling at him.

'Sure! A've jist come off channel ten.'

Emile smote the armchair. 'It was tonight!'

Hugh raised his head in acknowledgement. 'We arranged for tonight and she said she'd start broadcastin' as soon as she was ready.' He sighed. 'Poor lassie couldnae wait till A digested ma food.'

'And did you tell her?' Emile demanded.

'Tell her what?' I asked.

'Hugh was going to tell her that she must tune the television to another channel, just for a change.'

'A did mention it,' the Scotsman claimed, 'but it seems the bloody thing is fused solid on ten.'

In the days that followed the first of his appointments with Yvette, Hugh seemed irritated when I asked about her. That puzzled me since she was such a close neighbour and not easily ignored by either of us. 'Why are you so touchy?' I asked.

'A'll tell ye how! It's because you want tae know what kinda *person* she is. An' if she seems *happy*, for God's sake. Ye never ask me if she's a good *shag*!'

I considered the point for a moment. 'That's because I assume she must be a good shag, to draw so many admirers.'

'There! Ye see! "Admirers".' Against his better judgment, he laughed. 'They're no admirers. They're blokes that reckon they're ontae a good thing.'

'I don't see how that prevents her being a person,' I said.

For a few minutes we continued to undress in silence. It was another hot sticky night and the traffic sounds from the street rose sharply to the wide open windows and through the slats of the venetian blinds. When he was quite naked Hugh switched off the light and went to sit at the window in an effort to cool his body before trying to sleep. The illumination from the street filtered through in bars of light and shadow. Hugh lit a cigarette. 'Dae you no' fancy havin' a go, next door?' he asked.

I joined him at the window thinking that now might be the best time to let go of another secret. 'No. That isn't a big attraction for me.' Squatting on the camp stool I stretched my neck to rest my head against the cool wall.

'She's a good enough lookin' woman.'

'Oh, yes. She is.'

'Well, then, why no'?'

His cigarette smoke hung briefly between us before being sucked out in thin slices. 'I'm no use to anybody at the moment,' I said.

'Christ! Are you goin' tae make a confession?' he demanded.

I laughed. 'I suppose so.'

'Ye've come tae the very place.' He stubbed out his cigarette and twisted the blind round so that it formed a louvred screen between us. 'Let's do it right. A don't suppose ye've been tae confession before.'

'No, I haven't.'

'Okay. You say, "Bless me, Father, for I have sinned".'

I protested, 'But I haven't sinned.'

'Every bugger has sinned,' my confessor asserted smugly.

'But in my case the point is why I have not . . .'

'Say it.'

'"Bless me, Father, for I have sinned."'

'Blah, blah, snore . . . blah, blah, my child. How long has it been since your last confession?'

'I can't remember.'

'Cannae remember? Ye're due in this box once a year, at the very least. "Easter or thereabouts", mister – what the hell's kept ye?' The figure behind the screen bridled with indignation and abruptly pulled his balls into a more comfortable position. 'Go on.'

I wondered if I should. Obviously, Hugh had already made up his mind on what I was about to tell him and employed this charade as a means of easing the situation. He sprawled back in the armchair. His normally pink body was made curiously dark by the reflected light of the sodium street lamps. He still held the screen at right angles between us but now made it double as a sort of punkah, brushing over my knees. But if I didn't take this opportunity to tell him, the misunderstanding would create uneasiness and irritation. I began, 'You may think it very strange . . .'

'Not in the least,' he said quickly.

'But soon after I arrived in Montreal I discovered that I'd become . . . impotent.'

Clearly this was *not* what he'd expected. He sat forward, letting go of the blind which swung back, clattering against the window frame. 'Christ almighty!'

'I've been to a doctor, of course. He told me it won't last; that it often affects men at my age; that in my case it's probably caused by anxiety or strain.'

'Men at *your* age?' Hugh echoed. 'But that's *ma* age!'

I smiled. 'Yes, that's what I told Otto. In fact he's the only one I have told, so . . .'

'Why'd ye tell him? Unless he had occasion tae notice?'

There was no disguising the sharp hostility in Hugh's voice and I reeled slightly at the force and implication of the question. Though aware of exactly what he meant, I parried, 'What do you mean?'

'Well, ye're always talkin' aboot Otto, d'ye realise that?' He got it out in a rush. 'Otto did this, Otto said that – so, A jist wondered if maybe ye had tae tell him because maybe he wanted an explanation.'

'That's what you thought, is it?'

'Aye! That's what anybody wid think.'

I knew there would be no good – at that moment – explaining to him that the reason I'd told Otto was to find out if impotence figured in his research on the crisis year of twenty-seven. He'd confirmed that he knew of one or two such cases but thought my disability was more likely due to my anxiety at deserting the ship. To Hugh I said, 'I told Otto because I was worried; and he was a friend.'

'Then A wish tae God ye hadnae told me!' He lunged out of the chair and his bare feet went slap, slapping the whole length of the room.

'It was to explain my lack of your interest in Yvette. Why shouldn't I tell you?'

He turned and came swinging towards me, the bars of light sliding over his body. 'Because it makes me feel uncomfortable. Guilty, even!'

'Guilty?'

'Sure! How else could it be – wi' me prancin' aboot here wi' a hard-on whenever the notion takes me?' He positioned himself behind the armchair and I laughed with relief at realising the exact nature of his concern. On other occasions it had been difficult to avoid noticing that he was a man who was easily roused, but it had not occurred to me that his ready erections might worry him. Yet there he was, sheltering behind the armchair and defending himself against the charge of involuntary boasting. I laughed at the sheer arrogance of it. And my laughter seemed to reassure him more than any amount of talking. His shoulders relaxed and he smiled. 'It's no' somethin' A can *help*,' he said.

'Of course you can't! And I promise I will not be the least bit envious even if you become priapic.'

'Is that a permanent hard-on?'

'It is – and I think you're heading that way.'

'Balls!'

'As well,' I added.

Hugh strode away and threw himself full-length on his bed. I followed and lay down on mine. For many nights the heat and humidity dictated that we slept without any bedclothes. Indeed, the point of contact between neck and pillow was often insufferable. But now Hugh made a tentative gesture to reach to the foot of his bed and pull up the sheet. Then, aware I was watching him, he exclaimed, 'What the hell!' and threw it back.

I murmured, 'When I recover we can have a competition, if you like.'

He grunted, 'A don't know how ye can take it so easy. If ma prick wisnae workin' A'd be shattered.'

'Quite right!' I assured him. 'If my brains weren't working I'd be shattered, too.'

He threw a pillow at me and we left it at that.

SEVEN

For a few weeks around the middle of summer it seemed that nothing could go wrong. We kept our places and comfortably filled the roles which we'd chosen or which had been assigned to us. But I was aware of how we'd widened the nature of identity. Hugh and I, Emile and Paul became interchangeable as expressions of a carefree life which was full of activity, of coming and going, street and stair, dining-room and upper room, plans laid and expeditions accomplished, laughter and trust that all would be well. I was also aware of being happy while the happiness was going on. Until then happiness for me had always existed in retrospect. The city contributed a great deal to this afflatus. With all its faults and perhaps, in part, because of them as well as its many virtues, Montreal is capable of surging vitality; a sort of 'can do', give-it-a-whirl positiveness which night or day keeps time with whatever enterprise for good or ill that is demanded of it. And whereas I did not make any taxing demands for myself I did enjoy whatever occupied the time and attention of the other three.

The door to room five was rarely closed for long and whichever of us came or went always swung it a few times to encourage cooler air to circulate. In would come Paul with his portable drawing-board and a new design sketch on which he needed an immediate opinion. The telephone in the corridor would ring and a moment later Emile would enter like a Herald from the Greek camp with news from one of the others that a plan was changed or another bizarre outing had been devised. Hugh returned from press conferences or Expo duty full of high spirits and new deadlines. And, more often than was wise, I too arrived to find another of us there and eager to hear a full report.

As well as establishing a duty roster the wall calendar became an open appointments diary for all of us. Increasingly I noted that Emile seemed to be spending less time at his martial arts classes and more time at unspecified 'meetings'. When I asked him what was the purpose of these meetings I immediately wished I hadn't. His bright open face showed a flash of vivacity then clouded just as suddenly with embarrassment. 'These are *fairly* secret things,' he said uneasily, as though if I pressed him even a little he would reveal all, even to his own detriment.

'I'm sorry. I didn't mean to pry.'

He shrugged. 'It is not what you would like.'

It was difficult to make sense of that without further questioning so I just changed the subject, much to his relief. But it was clear that the meetings he attended once or twice a week were serious as well as secret. He prepared himself for them and took with him a businesslike folder. To my astonishment he was sometimes joined by Jean-Pierre. When I saw them hurrying away together I drew Hugh's attention to the unlikely partnership. 'Do you suppose it could be something illegal?'

'No' as far as Emile's concerned.'

'But with Jean-Pierre! What would interest him that *isn't* illegal?'

'If it's somethin' we should know we'll be told,' said Hugh and went back to his typewriter.

'Emile says it's something I wouldn't like,' I reported.

Hugh gave an eloquent grunt of amusement to indicate the wide range of possibilities this offered and went on typing. He was coping with a sudden flood of work in supplying background material and local colour to the UK for the imminent visit of Elizabeth II and Prince Philip to Canada. They were due at the end of June to join in the Centennial celebrations. They would also visit Montreal and Expo. Stands for cheering crowds had already been erected on the site and Hugh had staked himself a good position for the event. 'This is the kinda stuff that can be written in advance,' he said.

I buttoned a clean white shirt. 'What if she doesn't turn up?'

'No chance! Her Britannic Majesty always turns up,' he growled admiringly. 'She's a pro.'

'She is English, you know,' I reminded him.

'Only on her faither's side.'

'What's happened to your anglophobia?'

'A'm keepin' it warm,' he said. 'But anybody that can dae their job as well as she does hers could be an Ulster Redhander and A'd overlook it.' He glanced up as I moved towards the door. 'Where are you away tae?'

'A concert, in the Place des Arts.'

'By yersel'?'

'Unless you want a cheap fix of Brahms?'

The city's large arts complex reflected not only the wealth of Anglo-American business but, insofar as it could be managed with modern architecture, French good taste. And that was true in general of the thriving artistic life of Montreal. What was best was a product of French culture and it was paid for as a by-product of the commercial stranglehold which British and American companies showed no sign of relaxing. The Brahms concert was not a full-dress affair. That would have been far too expensive for me. In fact it was a fairly unreal public relations exercise for the guest conductor who'd agreed to open a late rehearsal to students and suchlike deserving persons. He addressed us with a great deal of synthetic charm and made himself available for many press photographs with studied spontaneity. Eventually, however, the orchestra did play real Brahms and I enjoyed the music.

Afterwards, since it was a mild summer evening, I decided I would walk back to the east end. Many other people had the same idea and for a while the sidewalk was well populated as we moved past the all-night drugstores, delicatessens and even all-night used-car lots, brightly lit and ringed by strings of little triangular flags. Gradually, though, the other strollers reached their destinations and the premises along the road changed to dark factory buildings defended by high chain-link fences. Some of them were also defended by dogs which kept pace with me, padding along in the shadows, sniffing and occasionally snarling.

I'd already walked quite a distance when I came abreast of a gap site on which several cars were parked. Oddly, some of them had their parking lights on. In the far corner of the site I could just make out what looked like a large workmen's hut. As I passed, the door opened and beyond the silhouette in the doorway I glimpsed a group of men standing around a table. The man in the doorway evidently heard my footsteps for his head jerked to an alert angle and he stared out into the darkness. He turned and shouted something to his colleagues then started out across the rubble-strewn waste ground in my direction. I glanced back and saw that others were following him. Their feet pounded behind me and I started to run. The sudden burst of activity roused the dogs in the adjoining factory site. They raced along with me, barking. Then the running footsteps were very close and I felt fingernails scratching my neck as the closest pursuer grabbed at the collar of my shirt. I wrenched myself free but in doing so stumbled against the wire fence. Three men closed in upon me. I steadied myself with my hands behind me then snatched them away as I felt a dog's wet muzzle on my fingers. A car veered across to the wrong side of the road so that its headlights blazed upon us. And now, as I was searched and various items examined, I could see that my three captors were all men in their late twenties or early thirties, smartly if rather flashily dressed. Since they seemed to be so interested in my identity I told them who I was. The sound of my voice, or my accent, seemed to reassure them. Those holding my arms relaxed their grip and the man who'd searched me leaned forward. 'We are sorry,' he smiled. 'This is a mistake.' Holding my wallet he moved closer to replace it in my hip pocket but in doing so he jerked his knee sharply towards my groin. As I felt the start of the movement I twisted my body and the blow pummelled the inside of my thigh. The car driver revved his engine and all three men got into the back seat and were driven away.

Considerably shaken, I continued my walk and had not gone more than fifty yards before I heard another car screech out of the waste ground and felt it catch me in its headlights. It slowed on the other side of the road from me and the driver shouted something in my direction. I stopped but could not make out what he was saying. Then the rear window of the large gleaming car was rolled down and to my astonishment I heard Emile's voice calling me, 'Bill! We give you a ride.'

I stood right where I was, so the young Frenchman got out of the car and crossed the road to reassure me.

'Those other guys make a mistake,' he said. 'When they hear you running away from the shed they think you are someone who has been listening.'

'I was nowhere near the shed!'

The car driver beat a rapid tattoo on the horn.

'Come now, anyway,' Emile urged me. 'It is still a long way.'

We crossed the road and the back door was thrust open to admit us.

There were already four tough-looking young men in the car who all reeked of deodorant. That was not surprising. As soon as the warm weather arrived I'd discovered the predominant smell in Montreal was a compound of deodorant and incinerator fumes – since burning was the preferred method of garbage disposal. Emile squeezed closer to the centre of the back seat to let me in and the car lurched forward as the occupants resumed their voluble discussion in Québécois. Emile joined in the discussion, though probably in French. He did not address any remarks to me and, intuitively, I guessed that speaking English in that company would have been tactless, if not down-right offensive.

Before long we reached a more residential area of the east end and Emile tapped the driver on the shoulder. The car stopped at a small coffee-house and the three of us on the back seat got out. Apparently this was an habitual calling place, for the proprietor seemed to know and be expecting Emile and the tall man who was with us. He was introduced to me as Claude, though he looked as far from the English connotation of that name as one could get. He was dressed entirely in black leather and had a leathery pock-marked face dominated by a high-bridged nose in which the bone threatened to break through. And he, too, carried a folder identical to that which Emile now laid on the table beside his coffee cup.

'It was lucky I saw you,' Emile said. 'Where were you walking?'
'From the Place des Arts.'

Claude glowered at me and spat out a question.

Emile responded with a tight little smile and shrugged, but he did not translate the remark which I partly guessed was to ask if 'Place des Arts' was *all* I could say in French.

I asked Emile, 'How did your meeting go?'

Before he could reply Claude delivered a rapid-fire injunction which indicated that, like others I'd met, he understood English perfectly well though claiming ignorance of the hated language.

Emile said, 'It went okay. We talk about some very technical matters.'

'Like revolution?'

Claude again censored whatever Emile might have replied to that and we sipped our coffee in silence.

Several other fanatical-looking young men came in to the cafe and greeted Claude softly as they grouped themselves round another table. Before long they called him over. He went readily enough but not until he'd delivered a whispered warning to Emile. When he was out of earshot I said, 'Judging by Claude your meetings can't be much fun.'

'No,' my young friend conceded, 'but they are important.'

'To you?'

'For the people here.'

'The French-speaking people, of course.'

Emile stared at me with troubled earnestness. 'It is their province and could be their country. Soon.'

That removed all doubt on the nature of the meetings and the purpose of the company we were keeping. It was a cell of the Quebec Liberation Front. Or perhaps a particularly militant splinter group of that organization which was determined that Quebec should break away from the rest of Canada to become a sovereign state. All through the sixties the momentum and urgency for that final break had been growing. That Quebec was large and resourceful enough to stand alone there was no doubt, but the power and influence was still held by the minority – the Anglo-American 'ascendancy'.

Emile asked, 'Were they rough when they stopped you?'

'I got the impression they were prepared to be. It was my accent which seemed to improve my chances – for a change.'

He nodded. 'Ah, yes. The spies who work for the fédéralistes and the vendus are all Canadians.'

'Spies?' I was incredulous that any of this activity could be going on in Britain's staid and friendly old colony.

'Spies, of course,' Emile asserted rather impatiently. 'Quebec is a very rich province and Montreal is the funnel through which most US dollars flow. The federal government will do much to hold on to it. And some things that are not nice.'

'What, for example?'

'Many dirty tricks which are hidden.'

'I didn't know you were interested in politics.'

He gave me an offended look. 'I am not. But I like the idea of freedom. The secret Résistance.' He leaned over the table. 'To be a member of the new Maquis.'

I nodded. Clearly the notions of danger and romance would have a magnetic appeal for the young Frenchman; though I could not see any close connection with the anti-Nazi guerrillas in occupied France.

When I told Hugh that we were harbouring a member of the new 'maquis' he said, 'Good for him!'

'But what if they involve him in some bombing or robbery?'

'As long as he has the sense no' tae run away he'll be all right.'

'He could get injured.'

'That would be better than gettin' intae the hands o' the polis – or the Insurance vigilantes.'

I stared at him incredulously. 'What?'

'Oh, aye! Far better tae get buried in the rubble than run away fae an explosion in this town.' He emptied his ashtray into a small metal bin. 'Anybody on his feet that's movin' faster than a brisk walk is sure tae get lifted – even if there's *nae* explosion!'

'Maybe the police are on the side of the Liberation Front.'

Hugh shook his head decisively. 'They're on naebody's side but their own.' He switched out the light and as I settled back to sleep I thought about the menacing figure of Claude, humourless and dedicated. No doubt even at that moment there were many others like him throughout the city and the province, returning from, or setting out upon, clandestine errands to raise funds, to plot strategy or to take reprisals. The hundredth anniversary of the federation of Canada could be the year which split it apart. As well as the splinter groups and violent activists there was already strong and legitimate support for the separatists movement. The Parti Québécois had steadily built up its following. The machinery was ready. Change was in the air and Montreal was the perfect place for sudden violence to trigger the decision.

Preparations for the royal visit still kept Hugh in a constant flurry of activity; attending briefing sessions, soliciting interviews, writing articles and logging reverse-charge calls to UK editors. Mostly these calls had to be made at five o'clock in the morning to bridge the time difference and, since he couldn't wake at that hour without an alarm, I woke too. That meant that there was more than two hours before breakfast to fill, so we made a virtue of a necessity and often went out for a walk between dawn and sunrise. Even that rundown part of the Maisonneuve quarter seemed beautiful then, and was cool. The main roads freshened by the water-trucks were practically empty. Dislodged by time and circumstance I think we both felt able to relax in a kind of brightening limbo. I assured Hugh that I did not really mind being forced out of bed so early.

'Sam didnae mind, either.' Seeing my puzzled look he added, 'A used tae get him up every mornin' tae borrow his bike – that was for the papers, tae. But A wis sellin' them then, no' writin' them.' He went on to explain that in order to get down to his paper-round it was necessary to have transport out of the vast housing scheme where nobody would think of having papers delivered to them. The newsagent did provide a proper bike for use on the round itself but that was kept in the shop and had to be returned there. Sam, however, had a bike of his own.

'Couldn't he just give you the key to the shed?' I asked.

'What shed? There were nae sheds! It was hard enough

keepin' the bloody houses held thegither.' He chuckled at the very idea. 'Christ, anybody that put up a shed in that three-storey concentration camp wis lookin' for a bonfire. Naw! Sam kept the bike in his lobby and A used tae chap him up each mornin' tae go doon tae the shop.'

'What age were you then?'

'Eleven. Naw, A must have been twelve because Sam wis gonnae get a start as apprentice the very week A lost his bike on 'im.' Hugh stopped in the middle of the sidewalk and turned his head while he pressed his fingers against a mark on his temple. 'See that!' I moved back to him and examined a long, faint scar which rose from the corner of his left eyebrow to his hair. He said, 'That's all there is tae show for a brand new bike that wis supposed tae get Sam tae his work.'

We walked on and I learned that Hugh hadn't exactly lost the bike. It had been forcibly taken from him by a rival 'team' of adolescents, one of whom had lashed him across the head with the detached guard chain. And the hijack had been well planned. They'd waited until he was coming back from the paper-round so that he was on foot and pushing the bike uphill. And they waited until Friday so that they could also take his week's wages. Hugh recounted these events with a kind of grim humour and told how, when he'd recovered enough to walk, he staggered back to Sam's house, blood pouring down his face but not caring about anything other than the fact that he'd lost the precious bike.

'An' ye know, he never blamed me!' The Scotsman's voice declaimed the joyful fact to the empty wakening street. 'No matter what it mean tae him, he never blamed *me*.'

'But didn't the police do anything?'

Hugh stopped again and weaved his head as though dodging slow arrows of incredulity and impatience. Then wearily he smiled across the gulf of ignorance which separated him from this middle-class Englishman who seemed to stand only a few paces away. 'Holy God, Bill, the "police"! They werenae for *us*! They're for people like you; tae protect ye fae people like us.'

'They don't seem to be very good at it,' I said.

He inclined his head sharply forward and we headed back to

do justice to the plentiful and delicious breakfast we knew would
be waiting.

A couple of weeks after the Brahms concert Emile came back
from one of his meetings in a state of great agitation. 'I must
talk to Hugh,' he declared.

'I don't know when he'll be back,' I said, then looked more
closely at his drawn and worried expression. 'What's wrong?'

'It is a very serious matter,' the young Frenchman assured
me.

'Is it something you must tell him tonight?'

'No. Not necessary tonight, but I would like to.'

'Okay. I'll let him know when he comes in.' I glanced at my
watch. 'You're back earlier than usual. Did Claude run out of
jokes at the coffee shop?'

He continued to stand irresolutely at the open door. 'Tonight
I did not stop at the coffee shop. And I have finish with Claude.
I have finish with all of those people.'

Though glad to hear it, I was non-committal. But it struck me
as very odd to see Emile so tense and depressed. We had come
to depend on his unfailing brightness and energy as a sort of
gauge by which we could measure the state of our *own* spirits.
He came further into the room then, catching sight of the
calendar, moved quickly to it and crossed out several entries
with emphatic strokes. That done he turned sharply about and
marched off to his own room.

About an hour later I heard Hugh clumping rather unsteadily
up the stair. When he reached the top, Emile's door opened and
he went in there first. He then reported to me that Emile wanted
to know exactly how the Scotsman planned to cover the royal
tour of Expo.

'Why did he want to know that?'

'A think he's feart some loony extremist is gonnae bomb the
procession.'

'Maybe he has good reason to think so.'

Hugh smiled and shook his head. 'They widnae be so daft,'
he said then, swaying slightly, started undressing with one hand.

'What did you tell him?'

'That A'll go where A'm put an' A cannae stay away.' He now discovered that his left hand still had some life in it and tried using both hands to pull the shirt over his head without unbuttoning. 'The nice thing is,' he mumbled from the tangle of his crossed arms. 'the boy's no' that worried aboot her Britannic Majesty – it's *me* he wants tae save.'

'Yes. Well, he probably knows you better.'

'True enough.' Hugh discarded the shirt and slumped on the edge of his bed.

'Even so, shouldn't you do something about the danger to others?'

'There's nae *danger*, A'm tellin' ye!' He allowed himself to fall back across the bed.

I waited to see if he had any immediate plans to complete the undressing but he soon dozed off and I put out the light.

Emile quickly recovered his former carefree manner. Indeed, just one night's sleep seemed to free him from the burden of liberating Quebec; and the memory that he'd ever wanted to do so. And since Hugh had not been at his most alert when warned of the possible danger at Expo, the whole matter slipped his mind as well. Jointly they were more preoccupied with devising a method of breaching the barrier of direct access to Yvette's flat. Madame Girard had the opportunity to inspect the fittings every Thursday when she changed the sheets and any tampering would have to be very subtle to elude her scrutiny. The main problem, as I understood it, was that the door was designed to open into room five and so the concealed hinges were on Yvette's side.

'So,' I said, 'screwing and unscrewing would be just as inconvenient as using the back way.'

Hugh chose to misinterpret, 'A don't think Yvette fancies buggery – an' A've never tried *un*-screwin'.' He turned to Emile. 'Have you?'

'It would take a long time,' the young Frenchman replied, not having understood the question.

We all gave our attention once more to the immovable steel bar and the slip-proof hasps which secured it in place.

'There must be another inter-connecting door,' I said.

'Not to me,' Emile shook his head sadly.

'What aboot Carlo's old room?' Hugh pressed him.

He shrugged. 'Behind the wardrobe, maybe.'

'But that room's locked up now anyway,' I reminded them.

'Sure. But what's tae stop Emile askin' for a shift?'

Emile seemed doubtful about that. Carlo's former room was the smallest of those on the top floor. However, he did ask Jean-Pierre for permission to view and later reported that the wardrobe concealed nothing but the predictable patch of unpainted wall.

At the end of the month the Queen arrived in Ottowa at the start of her visit to Canada which was marred initially by the fact that she had brought royal weather. Shortly before she got to Montreal, however, the authorities must have learned of the plans that Emile had heard only distantly hinted at. They took immediate, drastic and embarrassing action. Thus it was that the Queen of Britain and Canada was the one head of state whose safety could be guaranteed only by closing the entire Expo site to the public while she drove through it. The viewing stands were hastily dismantled or just left as empty and mute reproaches as the large black car nosed between silent pavilions in the rain. Jean-Pierre invited me down to watch that sad progress on television while, upstairs, Hugh angrily tore up the glowing reports he'd prepared in advance.

EIGHT

With a running advertisement, a regular appeal on a very popular radio programme and almost daily patrols on the Expo site we had little doubt that Sam would soon be caught. To these snares Paul added the idea of a permanent notice on the personal message-board at Dorval airport. Thus, instead of trying to get Sam before he left, it might be possible to get him as he arrived. The message-board was a free service used mainly by businessmen but in the official envelope Hugh placed exactly the same words as appeared in the *Montreal Star*. Paul himself undertook to make regular checks at the airport since it was not far from his girl-friend's house at Dorval.

For many weeks there was a feeling of high expectancy and tension on the top floor. Every 'phone call could mean only one thing; but always proved to mean one of several other things. Soon the strain began to show. Hugh's daily stint of four or five hours at Expo was wearing him down. The sheer physical exhaustion of staying on his feet, jostling through massed holiday crowds in the stunning heat soon had its effect on his work output. In the evening he'd set up the typewriter, stool, ashtray and paper at the end of his bed then go and stand at the open window watching the people passing by and straining to see who got out of any taxi cab which stopped in the vicinity. Every time the telephone rang he forced himself into a state of expectation.

'Why don't you get up into the mountains for a couple of days?' I suggested.

'Next month, maybe,' he said without turning round.

'Well, at least cut down on your time at the site. There's enough going for you as it is.'

He continued to stare down at the street. 'A wonder if he came the night we were all out thegither.'

'I shouldn't think so.'

He faced me sharply. 'But ye *did* think so! And noo *A* think so.' His obsession revalued what he'd scoffed at before.

'It is possible, I suppose. But if he called and there was nobody here wouldn't he come back again?'

'If he knew who was livin' here, aye. But look oot there – it's like Argyle Street at the bit where it goes fae bad tae worse. An' this buildin'. An' they stairs, an' that lobby! Wid *you* come here twice for nae mair than curiousity?'

I had to concede the justice of this. 'No. In fact I wouldn't come here even once for curiousity.'

Soon after that, at dinner, I again mentioned to Hugh that he should get away and Paul suggested a visit to Quebec as a way of satisfying Hugh's evident need for a break and his own need for a good week-end with Helene. She had a cousin in Quebec that she could tell her parents she wanted to visit. And if Paul just happened to be driving his friends through that way, naturally he would give her a lift.

'Sure!' Emile said at once. 'I don't mind. She can sit beside me.'

'She will sit beside me,' Paul decided. He turned to Hugh. 'And I would like you to drive.'

Hugh thought for a moment then nodded. 'Why not?'

'Good,' I said. 'And I'll have two whole days here without interruption.'

Paul said he would arrange it with Hélène for the second week-end in July. But it didn't work out like that.

One day as I was about to go downstairs I heard and then saw someone I knew on the first landing. He was knocking at the

Girard's door. I drew back immediately and listened to the jumble of voices as the man spoke first to Madame Girard, then to her interpreter, Jean-Pierre. After a few minutes he went away and I heard the door slam shut. I went back to room five in a state of some agitation. The man was a junior agent of the shipping line I'd deserted.

There was nothing I could do but wait and hope that help would arrive before action was taken to detain me. There was no one else on the top floor. Hugh was at Expo and both Paul and Emile were at work. I paced about for more than half an hour, always listening for footsteps on the stair. Then it occurred to me that if the situation was as I feared, at least Jean-Pierre would have come up to play the gaoler. It was one of his best roles. But more than an hour went by without a sound. And the first footsteps I heard were taking the steps two at a time. That meant Emile.

I gave him time to dunk himself in a bath of cold water and then to change before I went to his cramped room. He was sitting at the open door of the huge empty icebox. The Girards used the top floor to store their old lumber as well as house their lodgers. 'Would you like some snow?' Emile asked, and scooped his hand along the frost encrusted cooling element. I shook my head and he rubbed the melting crystals on his forearms.

'I have just seen an agent of the shipping company,' I told him. 'I think they've managed to track me down.'

He stood up. 'What do you want me to do?'

'I'd like you to go down and see Madame Girard. You're the only one of us she'll talk to.'

'I'm the only one us she can *understand*,' he observed, reasonably enough.

'Yes. Try and find out what is going on and what they plan to do.'

Emile nodded. 'Okay. But I will need an excuse. She will be busy preparing dinner at this moment.'

'That's good. You can apologise for *another* interruption – as though you knew about the man at the door.'

Emile pulled on his sandals, smiling at the neatness of the

ploy. But there was another difficulty. 'However, I cannot apologise for another interruption if *I* am not interrupting for something. What can that be?'

Both of us thought for a moment. Then I said, 'You can tell her about your week-end in Quebec.'

'But that is not for two weeks yet.'

'She likes plenty of notice.'

'Though not so much that she forgets when it comes.'

'Go on!'

He went downstairs and I went back to room five. Not more than three minutes elapsed before he was back smiling broadly. 'It is okay. There is no trouble. This guy did not come for you. He came only to rent Carlo's old room for one of his men.'

I let myself fall back on my bed. But my relief was soon arrested. '"One of his men"?'

Emile nodded, still beaming at the success of his mission. 'That's all.'

'*I* am one of his men.'

'So? You already have a room.'

I sat up again and clarified the point. 'Whoever is coming to Carlo's room is probably someone I know, or who knows me, or knows of me.'

Emile's expression changed to one of deep gloom. 'It will not be easy to avoid him, here on the top floor.'

It would be impossible.

At dinner Emile and Hugh between them managed to pump Jean-Pierre for the information that the new boarder was due at the end of the week. We all lapsed into thoughtful silence as we ate steadily through the meal. Even the passing of Yvette on the outside staircase with her latest partner failed to distract attention. Jean-Pierre was bewildered by our lack of conversation and even Madame Girard peered round the kitchen doorway fearing that something had gone disastrously wrong with the food.

'What's happened to you guys?' her son asked.

Emile replied, 'We wish Carlo had not gone away,' and even

in my depressed mood I had to admire the artful ambiguity of that statement.

It was only then that Hugh asked the question which should have been asked much earlier. 'How long's this new man gonnae stay here?'

'Coupla days, maybe. Who knows with sailors?'

We brightened as though a spell had been broken and Hugh dug me in the ribs. 'Right enough. Ye know what sailors are!'

Emile led the way as we trooped down the hallway, calling in jubilant unison, *'Merci, Madame!'*

'Bienvenue!'

So it was – to the accompaniment of channel ten – that the trip to Quebec was re-scheduled and the seats in the car re-allocated. Emile was philosophical about being deprived of his jaunt. He confided loudly, 'It is better for Paul's sake that I do not go. It would be a great pity for him to lose Hélène.'

We left early that Saturday morning and tried to look very businesslike when the car stopped outside Hélène's house. When we'd picked her up and moved round the corner we stopped again to change places. Hugh moved into the driver's seat. Paul and the girl went into the back. She was a petite dark-haired girl with a vivacious manner and heavily made-up eyes. And she made it plain that there was no obligation upon Hugh or me to engage her in flattering chit-chat. All her attention was devoted to Paul. Apparently that suited him very well and I was interested to note that whereas his normal behaviour was earnest and sober, with Hélène he assumed a superficial identity. He became consciously amusing and, I guessed, 'charming'.

Quebec is more than a hundred and fifty miles downstream of Montreal with a mid-point break at Trois Rivières, so we did not arrive in the capital of French Canada until well after lunch-time. Having dropped Paul and Hélène at one hotel we drove on to another. Previously I'd only seen Quebec from the deck of a ship and certainly that had been more impressive than the view from the streets. Where the river couldn't be seen, the 'new' city reminded me of Birmingham, but where the river

could be seen, that alone compelled awe. The St Lawrence
which sweeps around Montreal is strong and wide and fast
enough but essentially flat. At Quebec it is stronger and wider
and faster and seems to fill its mile-wide banks so full that it
develops a camber, arching perceptibly in the middle.

Even after a long and very tiring drive Hugh had cheered up
considerably. I think the arrival in a city new to him revived not
only the memory but the active feeling that he'd enjoyed in other
places with Sam. Indeed, he became quite excited at being able
to stand in the porch of the Château Frontenac and his enthusiasm for seeing the tourist sights even persuaded me to get into
a horse-drawn calèche for a guided tour of the 'old' city. He
kept asking the coach driver questions and seemed genuinely
fascinated with the answers. I, who had never been anywhere
with a tourist before, was bored and slightly embarrassed. Hugh
detected my disapproval. 'Whi's the point o' comin' tae a new
town if ye don't see the sights?' he asked.

'Yes. But what good does it do?'

'What good?'

'They'll still be the same whether you see them or not and
you'll still be the same whether you see them or not.'

'Naw, naw! *They'll* be the same – but *A'll* be different.'

We clopped along without talking for a few minutes, passing
other brightly coloured calèches full of people pointing at things
beyond them. I wondered if he was right. Possibly he could be
changed in some way by exterior sights. And I could not be.
And maybe that was just a sign of another basic difference
between us. I had no right to disapprove. 'I'm sorry,' I said.
'My trouble is that I'm too . . . stodgy.'

'No. Your trouble is ye're too sure o' yersel. An' self-centred.'
He turned his head to look straight at me so that I could see no
offence was intended. 'It's the breedin' does that,' he added.

'Oh! How?'

'If ye're the only son o' an English, middle-class couple – the
world's supposed tae come tae *you*.'

'It didn't.'

'Naw, but ye waited long enough tae see if it would, eh?'

I smiled, 'Perhaps.'

He seemed a little unsettled that I did not angrily contest his assessment, but went on anyway to give the other side of the hypothesis. 'Where*as* – if ye're the only son o' a poverty stricken, workin'-class, Scottish couple livin' in a housin' scheme barracks, *any* change is an improvement. Escape's the first idea that grabs ye, no' the last resort.'

'I can see how that follows.'

But he hadn't finished with it. 'Holy God! A room-an'-kitchen wid fit intae wan o' your gairden sheds – and be in much better surroundin's at that!'

It was a great relief, for a change, to have a room to myself with a bathroom attached – all to be paid for by the refugee from the room-and-kitchen. At breakfast he was full of plans for yet more sight-seeing and tried to stir my interest by noting that not only did the English conquer the French on the Plains of Abraham but the victorious general was a scourge of the Scots as well.

'I didn't know that.'

'Oh, aye!' Hugh ladled yet more sugar into his coffee. 'Bonnie Prince Charlie's men had a lot o' bother wi' Wolfe. He didnae like Catholics, y'know.'

'Then why do you want to see the place where he won his greatest victory?'

'Because no' only did he win here, he died here.'

We took a taxi and paid our seventy-five cents admission to the site. The fortifications were very much like fortifications anywhere that has them. But along the parapet of the outer curtain wall there was a paved walkway which gave a magnificent view of the river surging far below. There were benches and there were trees to provide shade so, while Hugh dashed away to importune yet another guide, I waited on the battlements.

The arrangement was that later in the day one of us would 'phone Emile to find out if the man in Carlo's room had gone and if not, how long he planned to stay. Also, if it had been possible to avoid any mention of, or questions about, me. In any event Hugh, Paul and Hélène would return to Montreal on Monday whereas I might have to wait in Quebec for a day or two longer. When the Scotsman returned with all the information he could gather on how the French managed to kill Wolfe I asked him, 'When should we call Emile?'

'When we get back tae the hotel.'

'I hope he could find out the man's name.'

'What does his name matter?'

'I'd like to know if it's just coincidence that he was sent to Girard's. You remember that list Jean-Pierre was making up? Maybe he did enter the next-of-kin and passed it on to mine.'

'So what? It's no' yer father ye have tae worry aboot, it's yer employers.'

'Oh, no!' I assured him. 'It *is* my father I have to worry about.'

Hugh stared at me in amazement. 'What?'

I nodded firmly. 'Certainly. The shipping line just wants me for another year. My father wants my life.' Getting up I invited Hugh to join me in a stroll along the parapet. It was time he knew something of the idyllic existence he kept accusing me of deserting. As far as the Scotsman knew I'd jumped ship on a light-hearted whim in order to spend a year writing. That was far from the whole truth and missed the force which drove me to what had been a desperate expedient.

I'd been a diligent engineer. My promotion had been steady and not hindered by the fact that many of the chief engineers and masters under whom I'd served knew my father personally, or certainly by reputation. But there was one major drawback to being the only son of Colin Thompson Consultants. Implicitly, it had made me a future asset of the Company before I had time to become an asset to myself. And now the Company wanted to realise its asset. That's why I'd jumped ship. But for months before I'd gone over the side the pressure had been building up in a steady barrage of letters from my father insisting that I should now apply for and sit my Chief's Ticket. When I had that it was expected that I would at once leave the sea and join the business ashore. At first that had seemed a way of escape. If I could avoid becoming a certificated chief engineer, the asset would not be ripe and there would be no virtue in having me join the business.

At sea nobody depended upon me except the few and changing engineers with whom I shared the watch. All that was expected of me was the performance of well-defined duties which I was perfectly capable of performing. And by that means I moved from the position of Fifth to Second Engineer. I'd served on two ships as Second before the owners started edging me onto the next step. I suspected that my father was behind the employers' sudden interest in my welfare. They, however, advanced different reasons. By them it was posed as my duty to achieve the much coveted Chief's Ticket. That was what they had trained me for. They had vacancies for Chief but no vacancies for Second. Their system and scheme of promotion was seizing up because of my obduracy. If I did not wish to serve the line in its best interest then they did not see how they'd be able to retain my services; or, as my last Chief had more directly described it – they'd no intention of letting me become a cork in the arsehole of progress.

Against all this I could not effectively argue. I understood my father's hopes and plans. I saw the shipping line's point of view. And in particular I'd become aware of resentment on a very personal level from my colleagues who blamed me for holding them down by refusing even to try and move up. That was why in October of the previous year, when the *Lycomedes* emerged from the Great Lakes bound for the UK, I'd taken the opportunity of her slow but irreversible progress through the Montreal locks to escape.

'But what aboot yer writin'?' Hugh asked.

'That was the only other thing I thought I might be able to do.'

'A'm sure ye can,' he said quickly.

Both of us leaned on the low battlement wall and stared down at the flood of the St Lawrence. The ferry boats were like huge dinner plates skimming tenaciously in wide loops; starting out set squarely up-river and allowing for the fierce current to sweep them back directly opposite on the other shore.

'My father is not a man who'd let an asset slip away,' I said. 'And he has loads of unfair pressure on his side.'

'What, for example?'

'Ownership, care and maintenance, my education, training. All that. And more – his hopes for what's in my best interest as well as his own.'

Bemused, Hugh shook his head. 'A think ma folks were glad tae get rid o' me. A wis eatin' too much, for a start.'

'They want you to be happy, though!'

'Oh, sure! But that's up tae me.'

When we got back to the hotel I called Emile who told me the man was leaving after breakfast on Monday and that his name was Hammond. I did not recognise the name so probably it was just coincidence that the agent looking through the new list of short-stay accommodation in a city full of Expo visitors had picked Girard's. Yet I knew the report of the *Lycomedes* officer I'd met would have been passed on to my father's office in Leadenhall Street. My father would have acted upon it. And he would be confident that when, eventually, he tracked me down I'd be unable to withstand the pressure to conform. As we drove to pick up Paul on Monday morning I confessed as much to Hugh. 'Why should ye?' he asked indignantly.

'Because, as things are going, I'll have no alternative. I've spent nine months trying to write a novel. That was to be my proof. My new passport.'

'There are mair weys tae earn a livin' than bein' a novelist,' he declared flatly.

'Yes. But that's the only way that would make it worthwhile.'

'Seems tae me it's a very fancy kind o' freedom you're after.'

'What do you mean?'

He grasped the wheel more firmly and his mouth tightened into the grim line which I'd come to recognise as a sign that unpalatable home truths were imminent. 'Ye want tae break out – but no' too *far* out. An' even at that, ye'd like tae keep a line open on a comfy seat at the boardroom table. Jist in case!'

'I think that's . . . prudent.'

'Oh, aye! It sure as hell is *prudent*. But let me tell ye, unless ye cut that line and jump one way or the other, ye'll be hung oot tae dry.' He stepped on the brakes with more vigour than necessary. 'Remember A said so!'

Paul and Hélène tumbled happily into the back seat of the car and we set off for Montreal.

NINE

In Glasgow, early in July, Mrs Moira Gillespie received a cheque for two hundred dollars. It was to be spent, Hugh wrote, on her air fare to Montreal. Moira was astonished. In the eight years during which they'd been married he had never before suggested that she might care to join him – wherever he was – for a holiday. That was because he never stayed in one place long enough for her to catch up with him. He regularly sent money, of course, though usually in high-denomination banknotes. Very often she knew where he was, or had recently been, only by identifying the currency and the stamp on the airmail letters. She never wrote to him; partly because she didn't like writing letters and partly because it was uncommon that he should provide her with an address. Now she had money, invitation and address. Being an optimistic woman she thought that this signalled a crucial improvement in their marriage. She immediately made plans for the middle fortnight in August.

But really the whole proposition arose from nothing more than Emile's highly developed sense of romance and a trick he played on Hugh. The young Frenchman passionately believed that a wife was an entirely different kind of woman from any other sorts of women that might be encountered. Once he found out Hugh had a wife and knew that he wrote to her as though she were an older sister he recognised that something was wrong and accepted as his clear duty every effort to put it right. One evening after dinner he followed us into room five and began with a pitch which was as near to guile as he was ever likely to get.

'Hugh, it is a fact that you have made some money here?'

'Quite a bit.'

'And you would do something for me?'

'Ye want tae borrow money?'

'Yes!' Emile exclaimed as though Hugh had proved himself adept at clairvoyance.

'How much?'

'You would write a cheque?'

'Aye. If A can afford it.' Hugh moved back to the chest of drawers and opened the unlocked top drawer to pull out his cheque book.

'Two hundred dollars?'

'Okay.' As Hugh wrote out the cheque Emile turned to me, his eyes shining with incredulity at the ease of his success.

I began to suspect something odd was afoot and suggested to the Scotsman, 'Shouldn't you ask what it's for?'

Hugh ripped the slip from the book. 'No' if it's for a friend.' He proffered the money to Emile. 'There ye are.' Emile took it. 'Anythin' else?'

'No. This is proof of what I think. You are a good friend, but a bad husband.'

'What's that got tae do wi' it?'

Emile moved around the room, holding the cheque delicately at arm's length and waving it gently. He explained, 'If you can write a cheque for two hundred dollars and give it to me without question – then you can send it instead to your wife and ask her to come here.' He placed himself beyond the double hurdle of the beds. 'It is a fact that I do not need the money, but I am very romantic.'

'And ye're no' married tae ma wife!' Hugh said grimly.

'Somebody is. Who can it be?'

'Well, what you've got will no' dae *her* any good.'

I wasn't so sure. 'He could endorse it.'

Emile seized on that. 'Tell me "endorsit",' he demanded.

'You could write on it that the cheque is to be paid to Mrs Gillespie.'

Hugh turned on me. 'You're as bad as that mad bugger!' he growled but I could see he was considering the matter on which, to some extent, his self-esteem depended. 'Even for a holiday she couldnae live here, could she?'

'Maybe that is one reason you *come* here,' Emile suggested.

Hugh grinned. 'And sub-let,' he said, nodding towards me. 'But two hundred'll only cover a one-way trip.'

'That is what I carefully plan,' Emile told him.

'Ye realise ye're puttin' a nail in ma coffin?'

'Why?' The Frenchman feigned innocence. 'Have you made your bed in a coffin?'

'Okay, okay, A'll do it.'

Emile then tore up the cheque he'd been given and went to his own room for some of Hugh's beer with which to celebrate the triumph of romance over freedom. It surprised me that Hugh had given in so quickly and it was not until much later that a possible reason emerged. Meanwhile, it was obvious that he felt no great need to have his wife by his side and he'd already told me that her principal objective was to start a family. When I expressed the opinion that surely having a family must have been his reason, too, for getting married, he gave me a pitying look and shook his head. Apparently what he'd wanted was not a home but a 'home base'; a place he could come back to and recoup his strength, should that prove a passing necessity. He'd told Moira as much before they were married and, on the face of it, she had accepted the possibility while being secretly convinced that she would soon make him settle down because she would be able to summon children to the offensive. Hugh confessed to me that he'd known what she had in mind and was guilty only of pretending that she might win. So, in a game of bluff and double bluff they got married. And Hugh lived his life as he'd told her he intended to live it and she had nothing to complain of, but could not win.

'Don't you think that's very unfair?' I asked him.

'Tae me or tae Moira?'

'To Moira, of course!'

'Her time'll come. A'll no' always be in ma twenties, or thirties even.'

'Nor will she.'

'She's in her thirties already. She's five years older than me.'

'But she can't have much satisfaction from the marriage.'

'She doesnae need satisfaction from the marriage, yet. She's got a good job she enjoys, an' she's nae fear o' endin' up an old maid. Y'see, marriage comes intae its own when ye're older. That's when ye need it. That's when we'll *baith* need it – and it'll be there. We've put doon the deposit!'

'Seems to be a very tidy arrangement,' I said with a sarcasm which lacked conviction. For, though there must have been a serious flaw in his argument, I could not at that moment identify it. Unless it was in the missing children. 'But by the time you want to make use of the marriage it will be too late for her to have children,' I said.

Hugh had thought of that as well. 'True enough. But ye see A don't want children, and the only reason *she* wants them is to tie me down – prematurely.'

I nodded. That, too, was implicit in the arrangement. He had covered all the angles. Searching in my mind for anything that might have been missed in the overall assessment I found, at the bottom of the barrel, 'Love. What about love? Surely people get married because they're in love.'

'A'm sure they dae,' he said, 'if they're lucky. What ye've got tae remember is the people that *don't* get married because they're no' in love wi' anybody when they should be at their best. All they get for bein' so fussy is a lonely old age.'

Again I nodded. And I did find it reassuring that Hugh had apparently considered the subject in some detail. Now and then the thought had occurred that it was about time *I* got married. And at home, I knew, my mother was building a stock-pile of eligible partners for the enterprise. It was heartening to be assured that I wasn't obliged to fall in love with any of them just because they were there. Besides, the wife of a consultant engineer must surely be a different kind of person from the wife of a writer. When, eventually, I went back to England as a novelist even my mother would have to concede the slump in my value as a possible husband for the daughters of her friends.

Of course, there wasn't much danger of such a rapid depreciation in my stock. And the distractions of life on the top floor had not improved my chances of plummeting out of favour.

The Greenock stories still refused to knit together as a convincing unit. Each time I devised a new method or link and persuaded Hugh to read the material, he liked it less. And each time he repeated what he'd said when he first read the stories, 'You're the wrong person tae write this.' It was his view that I should scrap the whole project and start on something like a diary of life in a public school, recalling lots of 'ripping wheezes' after lights out, or a fantasy about an ineptly modern Flying Dutchman. My ability, he felt, lay in dealing with arty ideas and not with real people.

'But I love these people,' I protested.

'Lovin' them will no' make ye one o' them,' he said with gloomy certainty.

'But that's exactly the point! That's what I'm trying to say. Don't you see?'

He gave me a bleak, though not unfriendly, stare. 'No. A don't see. And naebody else'll see, either.'

I took the sheaf of freshly typed paper he was handing back to me and, for the first time, began to have new doubts. The old doubts remained, of course, and were depressingly centred on my ability to do something that was worthwhile. The new doubts forced me to consider whether or not the enterprise *was* worthwhile. It was difficult to ignore the opinion of a man who was much closer to my subject than I; who had been born into, and brought up knowing intimately the inside of, the life which my novel could only describe from the outside.

Seeing the state of uneasiness he'd caused, Hugh broke off the excitable chattering of his own prose to observe, 'A'll say wan thing for ye, though – ye've got the accent right.'

'So have you!'

He grinned to acknowledge that even the one virtue he'd discovered had little value and applied himself once more to the celebration of Expo in the third person. Demand for his work was increasing. A whole procession of heads of state, trade delegations and cultural committees trooped in and out of Montreal. Armed with a comprehensive itinerary of coming events, Hugh was able to place just the right piece at the right time in their respective home markets.

Things were looking up, too, for Paul. He was employed as a technical illustrator by a company engaged in the manufacture of plant for the chemical industry. They'd recently won two large contracts on specifications which owed some – if not, in his opinion, all – of their attractiveness to the drawings of the proposed installations. The company had increased his salary but what was of more interest to Paul was the possibility of moving to a higher league in the USA by virtue of the evidence he could now offer to a new employer.

The success of my friends gave me satisfaction mainly because of the benefit they gained or were likely to gain. But it also underlined Otto's theory about the turning-point being reached. And I was beginning to realise that the nature of *my* turning point could be the turning from bad to worse. But before the truth of that was tested, I received a long letter from Otto.

He'd arrived in San Francisco with the intention of getting a job as a teacher but the spirit of the place and the times intervened. He became witness to the flowering of Haight-Ashbury. He encountered and became bearer to the tide of daffodils which promised to engulf the United States and lap against the 49th parallel. When he'd arrived no more than a month had elapsed since Ginsberg's Vernal Equinox and around the Golden Gate people knew that this year *everything* was possible. The war in Vietnam could be ended. It was possible. It was possible, too, for men to separate good from evil, beauty from ugliness. And surely hawks and doves must fly in different air. The race to destruction could be stopped because they would refuse to run. Setting an awful example to their elders, they would be content with smiling and sitting still; with smoking and loving; by so obviously possessing little of value and nothing to fear. And the voice of Hare Krishna was heard in the land.

What was most affecting about his letter was the sense of happiness it conveyed. A new joy in life seemed to be bursting out of him and he wanted to share it. Apparently he was already sharing a lot of it with a girl he'd met soon after he arrived there. He apologised for not writing sooner but too much had been happening. He also regretted that he could not give me an address to which I might reply because he was living a nomadic life, the path of which was untraceable by acid-hunting fuzz and distant friends alike. But he and his girl did plan to visit the World Fair and Otto estimated that with fair hitching and pauses along the way they'd get to Montreal by September. He said he hoped to see me then. I had no way of telling him that, almost certainly, he would not. Even with Hugh's generous help in cutting down my expenses all other prices were rising and my money would not last that long.

Since Otto's was the first letter I'd received at Girard's it aroused a fair amount of interest. It was natural that I should show it to Paul and Emile who knew Otto very well. My casual offer to let Hugh read it, however, was prompted more by a wish to demonstrate lack of evidence for his earlier suspicion than the courtesy that he should not be excluded. To my astonishment he seemed very much affected by what he read.

Handing the pages back to me he said, 'That sounds like a great guy. A wish he'd stayed *here*.'

'So do I. But if he had, we wouldn't be here.'

Hugh grunted. 'Right enough. At least A widnae be here.'

'Nor me. It wouldn't have been possible for *him* to pay for my bed and board as well as his own. Both of us would be elsewhere.'

This fact seemed to deepen the Scotsman's sentimental mood. He sighed reflectively and lit a cigarette. 'A wonder who we would've met, instead?'

'It's impossible to guess.'

'Aye. But they must exist.' He reached again for the letter. 'Let me see.'

I handed it to him and he skimmed quickly to a paragraph he'd found particularly relevant to his own preoccupation. 'Maybe A should have told *him* aboot the "witness".'

'He would have been very interested.'

'What made him go tae San Francisco?'

'He wanted to start his twenty-seventh year in a better climate and maybe more congenial surroundings.'

And, of course, Hugh wanted to know more about that crucial point of balance and change. I told him what Otto had told me and gave only a few of the examples from the uncanny list the

German had compiled of lives that had reached a turning point between the ages of twenty-six and twenty-eight.

'But they're all *famous* people – special. Maybe that's why it happened tae them.'

I shook my head. 'Being famous just means that somebody kept a record of it happening to them. It has happened to many others. I think it is happening to me – and you.'

'What's happenin'? What *is* it that happens?'

I thought for a moment. With Hugh, I felt sure, it would be unwise to go into any detail regarding the newly passive body and the access of spirit that could be achieved if apt preparation had been made. It was doubtful if he'd had the opportunity or the inclination to make any such preparation. 'What happens,' I said, 'is that your body stops growing and the potential for all you can ever be is set. Rather like the last fuelling port on a long voyage.'

He eyed me warily. 'The *last*?'

'Oh, you can stop at other places for other things – for food and relaxation and sight-seeing – but the ship will only go as far as the fuel it's got in the bunker tanks *now*.'

'So, ye have tae make up yer mind how ye want tae use it, eh?' I nodded and he pursued the idea. 'Which means if ye want tae go a long way ye'd better start goin' straight there.'

'As I understand it, yes.'

'But suppose ye want tae go a long way but ye don't know exactly where?'

'Then you make sure the tanks are full, and you get rid of excess cargo.'

'I'm all for that,' Hugh said, and grinned with the assurance of a man who'd spent his life shedding excess cargo. 'Did Otto tell ye all this?'

'Yes. Though he had other ways of describing it.'

'How did he see it?'

'As coming up to the edge of a very deep . . .' I paused '. . . chasm.' Hugh gave me a questioning look and I became eerily aware that the image I was about to describe had reached the Scotsman by other means long before this moment. He knew what I was going to say. But I went on. 'The choice is whether you get all your strength together and try to jump across that chasm, or just go back the way you came.'

'Or try to make a bridge,' Hugh said.

And that was it, of course. You could make a bridge if you had somebody to help you. I asked him, 'Did you really read *The Bridge of San Luis Rey* when you were a little boy?'

He gave a scoffing laugh. 'Not at all! A've *never* read it. Sam and I saw the picture at the Clydebank La Scala.' He stood up and stretched his arms. 'So, this is the last chance, eh?'

'This is the main one, but Otto claims there's another jumping-off point at the early forties.'

'Who the hell wid want tae jump *any*thing in their forties?' he demanded incredulously.

TEN

On the very warm summer evenings Montreal families lazed together on their balconies. There were whole areas of the city made up of quiet leafy streets of three storey brownstone tenements. And every flat had a balcony which was used as a natural extension of the living-room. Strolling along those streets was like walking through the stalls of an immensely long theatre in which a voluble audience had gathered and was growing impatient at the delay in starting the performance. They called up or down to each other between levels and conducted desultory shouted conversations across the street, through the curled leaves of the dispirited trees and over the heads of ambling pedestrians.

It was along just such a street that Emile led Hugh and me when the heat in the digs grew too intense on a memorable evening in July. During a recent visit to Expo we'd all steeled ourselves to enter what Hugh called 'the English brackets British pavilion' to find out if it was as ugly, ill-considered and fatuous as everybody claimed. And it was.

Emile said, 'I think this is because the English have no practice in trying to please anybody.'

'Except theirsels,' Hugh agreed.

I protested, 'That exhibit is not what *I* think of as *English*.'

A man's voice from a second floor balcony parroted the word, 'Engleesh!'

'Right!' said Hugh. 'It's what they think everybody *should* think is English.'

'Engleesh! Engleesh!' chanted two voices in unison from balconies ahead of us.

Hugh looked up to locate the calls. 'Ye seem tae be among fans here, anyway.'

'I do not think so,' Emile murmured, with the beginning of apprehension.

I responded to Hugh, 'Well, the exhibit should reflect their . . . I mean our . . .'

The interruption came in a heavily accented but clear child's voice, 'Fock the Engleesh cunts!'

Hugh shouted back, 'What *else* can ye do wi' them?'

But the listeners were not prepared for sophisticated reasoning and it was at that point the first few pebbles fell. Hugh was puzzled by the sound and stopped to glance behind him. Then a heavier fusillade was unleashed from balconies immediately above us. One stone struck Hugh on the chest and another, bouncing off the sidewalk, caught me just below the knee. Emile was hit on the shoulder. 'Engleesh! Engleesh! Engleesh!' The chant was taken up far ahead of us. We started to run. Emile put his hands on his head so that his forearms protected his face. Then we were hit by a concentrated barrage and had to stop and dive for cover behind an inadequate tree.

'Is this no' damnable!' Hugh spluttered.

Emile shrugged. 'They do not like the English.'

Hugh retorted angrily, 'But Holy Christ, you're a French separatist . . . and A'm a bloody Scotsman!'

'How can they know that, when we speak English?'

There was an odd feeling coursing down my spine and I put my hand to my back expecting to find it covered in blood. Instead I merely blocked a torrent of sweat which had its source between my shoulder blades and drained uncomfortably between my buttocks. The three of us were drenched, in an all-out lather brought on by the exertion of running even that short distance. The foliage above us was ripped by another fusillade.

'Where the hell dae they *get* the stones? On balconies!'

Emile, rubbing his arm, explained, 'They have plant boxes to grow flowers and so. The stones are on top of the soil for the sun should not dry it up.'

'I don't think it matters where they get the stones,' I said. It annoyed me that Emile seemed to be taking the outrage so calmly. Of course he had the comfort of knowing that they were not really throwing stones at *him*. And perhaps Hugh was willing to forgive the demonstration of people who so actively shared his own prejudice. What was clear to me was that the longer we waited the greater would be the stocks of ammunition held ready at both ends of the street. 'We'd better make a run for it,' I said. 'Maybe we could get away through one of those service alleys.' The others nodded. We put up our hands and forearms over our heads and dashed out. As soon as we were in clear view the stones came pelting down with sustained ferocity. I felt several blows and jabs but ran on, seeing only a few paces directly in front of me. When I glimpsed the corner of an alley I veered into it and kept running until I emerged exhausted onto another main street.

When I'd regained my breath I looked around for Hugh and Emile. But they must have chosen another alley. I started running again and was immediately stopped by a police car which crunched over the kerb directly in front of me with a door already swinging open. Foolishly, I thought they'd come to our rescue. The vigour with which I was hustled behind the grille on the back seat suggested otherwise. The officer who piled me in kept talking in rapid hectoring French and jolting my arm at each pause. I protested that I couldn't understand him. He grabbed my right hand and pulled a plastic bag over it and secured that with a rubber band before repeating the process on my left hand. That accomplished, the car bounced off the kerb and accelerated away from the mildly interested group of people who'd gathered to watch the arrest.

In the swift journey to the police station I realised that my first mistake was to be seen running in the street. They'd probably caught sight of me coming down the alley with my hands covering my face. Perhaps that had something to do with sealing my hands in plastic bags, though it could scarcely be from solicitude for the gashes and bruises I'd sustained upon them. The officer who still held me continued to question me in French but I kept shrugging and shaking my head. Surely they must know that *Lycomedes* was an English vessel. I decided it would be better for me to wait and talk to whoever the line agent sent to reclaim me.

The duty officer took out a thin, red-bordered folder which contained several long forms. My photograph was stapled to the top sheet. The duty officer glanced up at me then at the photograph and signalled that I was to be taken elsewhere. I was hustled into the car again for a short drive to a new looking building. The whitewashed room where they took me was small and furnished with a hard, white-sheeted, examination table, two chairs and several antiseptic-looking containers. In the corner was a portable shower set up on a curious rostrum which looked like a drain tank.

My new attendants said nothing but drew on new rubber gloves and began, very carefully, to strip me naked. There was some relief in being divested of my sweat-sodden clothes but my hands – still encased in plastic bags – were itching and aching at the same time. Every piece of my clothing was dropped into one of the antiseptic bins which was then sealed and labelled. Meanwhile I was urged into the shower. The water was tepid but delivered with great force. And, apparently, it was valuable. As soon as the shower started one of the officers opened a tap on the side of the tank on which I was standing and collected in a large drum, the water that had run off me. The drum, too, was sealed. I was then dressed in a hospital examination gown resembling a wrap-around pinafore and firmly pressed to sit down. My silent attendants loaded the labelled bin and drum onto a luggage trolley and wheeled it out, leaving me alone to consider how unwise it is to jump ship in Montreal.

But I wasn't given long to consider this. The door opened and a plump, florid-faced man in civilian clothes came in, followed by a young woman I took to be his secretary. However, she was already wearing rubber gloves and promptly opened a manicure case on the floor beside me. The man sat in the other chair and started talking to me rather boisterously in French. Several times I heard the name 'Armand'. Then it became clear he was addressing me as 'Armand'.

'I'm sorry,' I said, 'I don't speak French.'

He gave me an amazed look then smiled and nodded. 'Very good. Very *good*.'

'Do you think I am someone called Armand?'

'"Someone called Armand",' he repeated, chuckling at the audacity of this approach. There followed several hectic sentences in French which seemed to be made up entirely of consonants.

I stared blankly at him and the young woman, having arranged her manicure equipment and labelled two small glass phials, started to take off the plastic bags which covered my hands. She sealed those then scraped whatever could be found from under each of my fingernails in turn. She dug the implement well in and swept it round in a tiny arc with a firm efficiency that must have come from a lot of practice.

The florid-faced man and I watched the operation in silence. It was now obvious to me that I had not been arrested for jumping ship. I'd been arrested on suspicion of arson. My hand in the grip of the efficient young woman began to shake. Indeed, my whole body started shivering, partly as a result of the shower water cooling on me but more from simple, irresistible fear. To be an arson suspect in this city was about the worst thing that could happen to anybody. Everyone still held clearly in mind the scandal, now several months old, of the systematic beating-up and torture of a number of suspects carried out by a group of police officers and insurance investigators. No doubt it was the infamy of that which led to the elaborate evidence collection procedure I was going through. While they tested the clothes and the water and the nail debris, though, there was plenty of time for some good old-fashioned persuasion by the insurance investigator. When the young woman left with her instruments and samples he called in one of the policemen. They started a vivacious conversation behind my back which was full of exclamations, reiterations and some pointed pauses. Though I could not see, I knew they were watching me carefully. Their conversation was obviously designed to trap 'Armand' or at least to trap me into revealing that I understood what they were saying. Never was I more grateful for the cheerful ineptitude of language-teaching in English schools.

The insurance man dismissed his foil and sat down in the chair opposite me. 'So, you say you are not Armand – yet you knew the name.'

'I recognised the name. It was the only word I could make out.'

'You know Armand, then?'

'Only as a character.'

'Oh, he is a character all right!' He made a two-handed gesture of an explosion. 'Phoof! He is a character, no mistake.'

'I mean in *La Dame aux Camélias*.' I was anxious to ingratiate myself and added helpfully, 'He is her lover.'

For some reason this made the insurance man very angry. His round face tightened and glowed a deep red. He lunged forward and struck below my left ear with the edge of his rigid palm. My chair heeled over but did not topple. But immediately the man seemed to regret the attack, or perhaps he remembered the recent scandal. He gave a curiously wooden shrug of apology. 'This isn't a matter of love,' he said.

I shook my head in wholehearted agreement.

'Let us begin with the proper form. What is your name?'

'William Thompson. And there is someone I would like to telephone, where I live.'

'Oh?' His expression brightened. It was not often that suspects offered to locate accomplices. 'Write the address and telephone number. I will get someone to call there.' He gave me a pen and a label. 'And the name of the person you want to see.' He forced his face into a smile. 'As long as it is not "la dame aux Camélias".'

I added Hugh's name.

He handed the slip of card to the policeman waiting outside the door and came back with the red-bordered folder. 'This is your photograph?'

'Yes,' I said and noted, looking closer, that it was an enlargement of a holiday snap which was taken in Sussex a couple of years earlier. No doubt that had been the photograph my father had provided when I was first reported missing. Some of my confidence returned. If things were going to be done according to the book I now knew that, should it be necessary, I could secure my present release by pledging my future to Colin Thompson Partners. I asked the insurance investigator, 'Did you provide that photograph for the file?'

'No. It's a police photograph. They have all suspects under surveillance.'

'In England?'

'What?'

'I think they've clipped the wrong photograph to your file.'

'No chance!' he said, but I saw a slight suspicion in his eyes and, under the pretext of studying one of the many forms, he turned up the free corner of the photograph to look at the back. Then he continued going through the list of dates and locations and the well-documented enterprises of which Armand was suspected.

'There must be a written description,' I persisted. 'Have you read that?'

He pretended to ignore the question but I saw him turn to what must have been statements by witnesses. His expression did not change but after a few minutes he asked me to stand up. He stood beside me. That would establish whether or not my height corresponded with the reports. He pushed me into the chair again and suddenly delved at the hair on top of my head as though searching for lice, but probably just to determine if the roots were a different colour from the rest. He turned away. 'Yes. We'll see what your friend can tell us.'

I was then taken to a small interrogation cell and given a sort of combination track-suit to wear. Left alone and feeling fairly comfortable I began to take an optimistic view of my situation. The feeling did not last long. The door was thrust wide and on the threshold identifying me was not Hugh Gillespie but Jean-Pierre Girard. He looked frightened and nodded once. The door was slammed shut again.

Then it seemed hours went by while I saw myself being implicated not only in arson but in heroin pushing, murder, child molesting and any other unsolved crime they cared to clear up with the minimum of fuss. As a character witness Jean-Pierre had the edge on Judas Iscariot. My year of crisis was certainly taking full advantage of its potential. And everything hinged upon identity. Since I'd thrown away the person everyone else thought it suitable for me to be nothing had gone right. And punishments for taking pride in the person *I* thought I was came thick and unmistakable as ancient warnings of hubris. Impotence, lack of money, lack of talent, fear, humiliation and even casual stoning were thrust with me into the limbo I'd chosen. Staring at the backs of my hands and my forearms on which the gashes were becoming inflamed and the bruises deepening in colour, I began to realise that all the resources I'd ever had were gifts or loans from other people. My upbringing, education and training had all been designed to preclude my becoming a self-reliant individual. Except, perhaps, for those years in Greenock. I'd been sure of myself then. The people there knew for a fact that I was a separate person. A sometimes irritating, prissy, bumptious person, to be sure, but undeniably a whole and separate person. Thinking of Greenock cheered me quite a bit. No matter what tale Jean-Pierre might now be telling the Montreal police, I knew that I had enjoyed the real anger and the real trust of other witnesses. And, in a way, I still possessed proof of that.

After a long while a policeman came in to say that I was being held overnight. He took me back to the police station and along the wax-reeking corridor to a proper cell which had a bunk, a bible and a plastic-looking string of rosary beads which – someone told me later – would snap under immodest pressure and would melt in the mouth. This was to forestall the prisoner garotting himself or anyone else with them, or choking upon them to secure a move to hospital.

Apparently, the forensic department employed by the insurance companies worked twenty-four hours a day. Even at that, considering the quantity of evidence they had to deal with, it must have been a well-staffed and flourishing department resembling a small factory. Around eleven o'clock the following morning my clothes were returned to me – clean but ripped to pieces. I spread them out on the bunk and they looked like patterns for *making* clothes. Everything was there, but in 'kit' form. I stuffed the various pieces of material back in the linen draw-string bag which was emblazoned with the colourful Expo motif.

Another hour elapsed before I was brought out for another interview with the duty officer. He asked me to sign two forms, one of them a waiver of any claim for damages to my property. Then he warned me not to make any sudden moves away from the address where they could locate me. My impression was that he was more than a little embarrassed over the mix-up with the photograph. Yet he did not ask why the police should have my photograph at all. Presumably it had come from another department whose sloppy paper-work was not his business. He told me to sit on the bench opposite the desk. But almost immediately the 'phone rang. He picked it up, nodded, then told me, 'Your friend's waiting. You can go.'

It was Hugh who waited with a taxi. On the journey back to the digs he explained how he saw the sequence of events. When the call came from the police it was Emile who'd answered the 'phone. That was one of his self-imposed duties as the only expert French/Québécois speaker on the top floor. But since the officer was demanding to speak to Hugh Gillespie, the owner of the house, Emile had merely alerted Hugh and summoned Jean-Pierre to deal with an official enquiry.

'An' lucky for you that's who did speak tae them,' said Hugh.

'Lucky!'

'Sure. The sleekit wee bastard's a mate o' theirs, it seems.'

'You mean an informer. That's what I was afraid of.'

'Well, he came back pleased as punch last night wi' his wee folder. A'm tellin' you, we should thank Christ he's such a nosey bugger.'

'How did that help me?'

'Alibi!' Hugh thumped the cushioned seat between us in the taxi. 'Young J.P. has got every movement logged. He knows when we're in, when we're oot. Dates an' times – the lot! He wis able tae tell them that for months past you've been a bloody *hermit*. An' he didnae ask much for sayin' so?'

'Ask who?'

'Who else? Me.'

I gulped hard. 'He asked you for money in exchange for telling them . . . that I couldn't be held responsible for widespread arson?'

'Naw. No' in exchange. In reward. He did it first, then asked.'

'You paid him a *reward*! Why?'

'Because there might be other times.'

'They won't arrest me again.'

'They could. Or it could be me. And maybe no' the polis. Whatever it is, there's very few illnesses in this city that money wulnae cure.'

'How much did you pay him?'

'That's ma business,' said Hugh.

Back at Girard's, Jean-Pierre came out as we reached the first landing. Obviously he'd seen the taxi arrive and having received money now wanted applause as well.

'You all right, Bill?'

'Yes, thank you.'

'Anything else I can do for you?'

Hugh grunted and continued up the wooden stair.

'No,' I told Jean-Pierre, 'there's nothing I want but a bath and proper clothes.'

He pointed at the bundle under my arm. 'They ripped up your gear, huh?'

'They certainly did.'

He adopted his familiar bargaining stance. 'Ya like to give it to me I know somebody'd fix everything good as new.'

'Oh! Yes. Thank you.' I handed him the bag and followed Hugh up the stairs marvelling that in 'can do' Montreal there was, of course, a cottage industry devoted to restitching forensic damage.

ELEVEN

With a little back-tracking it was easy to work out how the false arrest had been managed. It was something the city's police frequently managed – just to be on the safe side. In my case their procedure was complicated by the fact that it was really two other agencies who were involved and the police were just providing the muscle. First there was the dock security force who circulated a photograph, then there was the private investigation branch of the insurance companies who circulated a dossier as complicated as one of their policies, but which had no photograph. Once the photograph had mistakenly been attached to the dossier in an office which did not deal with either of these things there was a natural inclination by those who received it not to read something which was so clearly illustrated.

For a couple of days after my escape I was foolish enough to believe that the unfortunate incident was closed. But I gravely underestimated the Montreal police. As soon as they found out that they did not have 'Armand' they wasted no time in finding out exactly who they did have. The source of the photograph was traced, telex messages were exchanged and more or less before my feet had touched the ground again Jean-Pierre tapped at the door and called, 'Bill! There's a guy here to see you.' It was in the middle of the afternoon and Hugh was at Expo. As I crossed the room I heard the courier's feet retreating quickly downstairs. I opened the door and found the 'guy' was my father. His impressive, rather portly figure was dressed in a light tan, carefully tailored, cotton suit. His crisp shirt had a mandarin collar and his leather shoes were as highly polished as ever. We shook hands and he moved towards the armchair at the window. He removed Hugh's trousers which were stretched over the back and placed them on the bed before sitting down. Without appearing to do so, I knew he was taking in every detail of the room, including the fact that both of the beds were evidently in use. I leaned against the child's desk backed by the large site-photograph of Expo. 'When did they tell you?' I asked.

'The shipping agents told me three months ago you were in the city. I was here myself at the end of May. Last night the London office sent a telex to me in Cleveland giving this address.'

'I'm sorry if you and mother have been worried.'

That clearly didn't require comment from him so he did not respond.

'I tried to warn you in the letters,' I began.

'*Warn* me?' He seemed faintly amused at the word.

'About how things were going.'

'Until you decided to stick at Second, things were going exactly as planned.'

'Exactly as *you* planned.'

He raised his eyebrows. 'I think it's unlikely you'd reach even Second without a mind of your own.'

'All right. Let's say I've changed my mind.'

He nodded and stretched his legs to cross his ankles, exuding assurance and prepared to be patient. He seemed to fill the room with sheer authority. If I'd thought he could only do that at home or in his office I was mistaken. He could do it anywhere. 'Why have you changed your mind?' he asked.

'Perhaps because *I* have changed.'

'You are thinner,' he observed drily.

'And more independent.'

His voice hardened. 'Yes. Breaking your legal obligations and deserting your ship certainly proves "independence", but nothing to boast about.'

'I wanted some time to myself,' I said.

He leaned forward and gave several sharp nods as though this was a childish misconception he'd often had to deal with. 'Yes,

yes. And you've had nine months. What have you done with it? Apart from lose weight.'

The tone and the question vividly reminded me of several occasions in my youth when my father returned from one of his many long trips abroad and called me into his study exactly half an hour before tea to explain what I'd done and how I had progressed in his absence. Half an hour was always too long for my brief recital. And I could not imagine *why* he'd be interested. 'Well?' His voice sharply probed the silence – and that was familiar too.

'Nothing,' I said.

He leaned back again. 'I think nine months to do nothing is a bit . . . indulgent, don't you?'

'It's not that I *intended* to do nothing,' I retorted. 'It's just that I have nothing to show for it.'

'Well, that won't do, will it? Particularly when it has cost other people such a lot.' He paused. 'You do see that?'

I nodded. There was nothing in what he said that was not just and sensible and I began to wonder if, secretly, I was glad to be rescued from an obvious folly. Perhaps the obligation I'd felt towards myself was an obligation merely to try but not, necessarily, to succeed.

My father, seeing that he'd won the argument, felt he could afford some idle speculation. 'What was it that you planned to do with the time you've taken?'

'I planned to write a novel.'

'Why?'

'Because people interest me.'

'All people, or just strangers?' He delivered the lightly sarcastic question as though the answer didn't matter in the least, but there was in it, too, the palest shade of regret for lost affection.

I shrugged. There was no way of amplifying my intention without increasing the offence. Instead I asked, 'How are things at home?'

'Much as usual.' He latched immediately onto a more pertinent question. 'I suppose there's no obstacle to prevent you coming back immediately?'

'I wish there were.' And I also wished that it were not so

easy to abandon the freedom I'd gone to such lengths to secure. Very clear now was the fact that what I'd feared and hidden from was not an exterior retribution but an interior weakness.

My father sighed. 'The shipowners are willing to take a lenient attitude.'

'For your sake.'

'What?' It amazed me how that simple word delivered in just that way was capable of plucking me back ten or fifteen years.

'They'd be lenient with me because of you.'

He nodded, seeing no possible grounds for objection in that.

There was a pause which I knew would have to be broken by me. 'How's the company doing?'

'Fairly well,' he conceded. That, I knew, meant it was flourishing like the green bay tree. He went on, 'But we will need another man in London, fairly soon.'

'How soon?'

'To start in the new year.'

I was taken aback. 'That's impossible. It would take me at least a full year to get my Chief's Ticket.'

'Yes. However, if you didn't come into the company as a partner we wouldn't expect a fully qualified chief. Partnership could come later.'

'How much later?'

'That depends upon you.'

'Oh, no. On *you*, surely! It's your company.'

'And will eventually be yours,' he said irritably. His patience was not inexhaustible. 'Provided you don't give way to any more idle whims, your place on the board is assured. It's just a matter of time.'

'And "prudence",' I recalled.

My father's expression brightened. 'I've always given you credit for that.'

'Yes. I've always had that. But recently I've wondered if it was worth having.' I became conscious of the bleak room in which we were discussing the person that I was intended to be, and everything about it denied the possibility. But gradually I began to gain strength from it and from the new identity I'd been assigned as one of the top-floor fraternity. There was still time to take a leap in the dark and I decided to do it. But it needed a short run up to the edge. 'I'm not sure I want to go back at all,' I said.

My father's hands tensed on the arms of the chair but he kept his voice relaxed. 'What *are* you sure of, Billy? Or how long will it be before you are sure?'

I adjusted my position against the edge of the desk and shook my head. Yet here, I knew, was my opportunity to set a bargaining position. 'I think I'll know by the time the World Fair ends.'

'October.' My father breathed the word, then, much more firmly, decided. 'Whether you actually know your mind then or just think you know it, October would be too late.' He stood up and looked out on the street. Both of us were now well aware that a decision in October would be too late not only for whatever projects the company had planned in the new year but too late for me to have any future in the company. 'I'd intended going back to London immediately,' he said without looking at me, 'but I could wait in Montreal for a few days more.'

Although there was no one else in the room but my father and I, it seemed to me that Hugh was watching and listening. He was intent on hearing what I would say next. Feeling myself decidedly in mid-air I said, 'Please don't wait on my account.'

My father nodded slowly, as though acknowledging people in the sidewalk below. Perhaps he'd already reached a conclusion about me before he'd walked into the room. Certainly the tone of my letters before I fled the ship, then the very fact of my desertion could have left little doubt of my reluctance to comply with his plans. Indeed, it must have occurred to him that I was no longer dependable enough to be trusted with his life's work. Still, he had tried to cram me into shape again and in spite of his misgivings he'd very nearly won. Typically, he wasted no time at all on what might have been. His attention moved to the next item in his list of priorities. 'Are you in good health?'

'Yes, thank you. And you?'

'Fine.' He turned now to look pointedly at the room. 'And . . . comfortable here?'

'It gets very warm,' I said.

'Yes.' His eyes focused on the two beds. 'Your mother will ask me if you are married, or planning to marry.'

I smiled and, for the first time, he smiled as we acknowledged the irrelevant preoccupations of the woman whom both of us held in great esteem. 'No,' I told him. 'No, on both counts.'

'And there's nothing more you want to say?' There was absolutely no rancour in his voice; no hint that I was betraying his longest cherished hope. Against my will I was filled with admiration for his unemotional acceptance of things as they were.

'I am very short of money,' I said.

'It's not surprising,' my father observed. 'But I'm not going to give you money you haven't earned.' He looked at me coolly and, noting that I was not going to quibble or plead, afforded some mitigating circumstances. 'If it's a matter of reasonable debt, though . . .'

I caught at it. 'There *is* a matter of reasonable debt.'

He took out his cheque book and came to lean on the desk. 'Yes?'

'Eight hundred dollars payable to Hugh Gillespie,'

He wrote it out before he asked, 'What's it for?'

'Board and shelter and ransom,' I told him.

He straightened up and handed me the cheque. Then from a side pocket of his elegant suit he drew my passport and laid it on the desk – rather as though he was cutting a deck of cards – explaining, 'I collected it from the agents earlier today.'

'Oh, good! That will be useful.'

With some difficulty he raised a point that must have been nagging him but which was not strictly relevant to our meeting. 'If you wanted to write a novel, why couldn't you write it at home?'

I smiled. 'I suppose because if I did it there it would have been no more than a hobby. Here, it was an alternative – and a necessity.'

'And a failure, you say?'

'So far, yes.'

He shook his head sadly. 'Seems a great waste of time.'

'Not entirely. I have persuaded you that I'm the wrong man for your job.'

'Yes.' His eyes regarded me soberly. 'Let's hope neither of us will regret that.'

'I'm sure you won't,' I told him. 'There's no way I could have measured up to what you expect of me.'

He touched my shoulder lightly. 'I didn't know it was such a burden,' he said.

'I know. And I'm sorry.' Staring at the floor I saw the expensive, highly polished shoes move away over the worn track in the linoleum. Then the door was firmly shut.

When Hugh got back just before dinner I told him about my father's visit and passed on the cheque. He was delighted to receive it. But he was now preoccupied with another visitor who would yield a bonus. The President of France was coming to Montreal. Already the white lines on the streets over which he would pass were repainted in the shape of fleur-de-lys. Officially Charles de Gaulle would be on a state visit to Canada, but no branch of the separatist movement spared any effort in harnessing the feverish excitement to make it a state visit to the province of Quebec. The federal agencies did what they could to combat such a dangerous idea. They got no help from France. The President would arrive not in Ottawa but in the city of Quebec and whoever was to meet him must meet him there.

Hugh rewrote his 'triumphal progress' pieces with a new cast and Emile translated them. They pounded away for hours together, with the young Frenchman in a high state of elation at finding himself so valuable. And now it was Emile who rose at dawn and conducted voluble telephone conversations with Europe. Indeed, Hugh gladly allowed him to become the senior partner in this particular enterprise and they shared the payment accordingly.

Paul and I were excluded from the high-power press work, and from the 'city desk' that room five had become. Since my typewriter had been bought in Montreal and had French accents Emile requisitioned it. He crouched over the keyboard, desperately stabbing away and shouting at me, 'I am busy. Go with the Genovese!' So, I went with the Genovese. And since there was no comfort in Paul's room we took many long drives in the Oldsmobile.

He was amazed at my decision to give up an assured position on the board of a successful company. 'It is strange that you refuse the thing that I am aiming at,' he said as he drove towards the spectacular St Joseph's Oratory.

'Are you?'

'Oh, yes! For many years everything I do is only for that. The training, the travel, the experience, the learning English . . .' Keeping his eyes on the approaching junction he grinned. 'Which is the hardest, as you can tell. All these things are so I shall be a respected director of profitable international business.' He turned the car westward onto Sherbrooke and added, 'One day.'

'I'm sure it won't take you very long.'

He gave a doubtful little shrug – more from modesty than doubt – and told me, 'Already I am twenty-six years old. But however long it takes I will do it.'

'In Genoa?'

'Of course! Who would not wish to be a successful man at home? Apart from you, I mean.'

'I think I'd rather be happy,' I said.

The car lurched as he gained precedence over a low-slung taxi. 'Bill, that is not sensible to say,' he protested. 'How can you be happy if you are a failure?'

'Ah! Well, I wouldn't let the happiness carry me as *far* as that.'

Fearing he had not understood the implications, Paul didn't comment. We continued in silence, skirting round the base of Mount Royal and climbing the Côtes des Neiges road. And before long we could see the soaring floodlit façade of the enormous church set against the theatrical darkness of the receding hill beyond.

Paul was a keen photographer and the Oratory was the object of our expedition. Certainly it was a notable tourist attraction and the long Palladian stairway to the entrance was bustling with people. Whether they were devout Catholics, or devout photographers, or both, it was impossible to tell. They all seemed to have cameras, though. Paul offered me the use of one of his but knowing it would be a waste of film, I declined. As he strode purposefully in and around the building I became fascinated by the rasping swarm of large insects which practically blacked out the clear-glass globes of the candelabra on the stairway. The variety of their species was astonishing. Some of them were the size of small birds. Their concentrated, manic circling and darting and the constant drone of their wings against the warm summer air provided hypnotic whirlpools of sound and motion. Why, I wondered – since insects are supposed to be so clever – could they not communicate to each other that there was no great virtue or reward in reaching the light? And surely they must notice that those who came too close died? Why, I asked myself, were there not more wise, *old* insects like Thurber's moth? With a certain smugness I quoted to myself, 'Who flies afar from the sphere of our sorrow is here today and here tomorrow.' When Paul dragged me away, I had not seen the church at all.

Evidently he had been thinking of what he saw as my problem. As we drove back, and without preamble, he stated, 'I think you must write to your father saying you did not understand what he meant – about the future.'

'He'd find that hard to believe.'

'Not if he *wants* to believe it. And, of course, he will. And he will forgive you. What father would not!'

It had not occurred to me that I might be in need of forgiveness, but then I was not a member of the large, warm Italian family which had Paul in its possession. Nor could I easily explain to him that my father would see my decision more as a reneged contract than a personal disappointment. And whereas my failure to deliver would impair our relationship quite a bit, immediate compliance would not have improved it much either. To Paul I said, 'My father is a very practical man.'

'This is a very good thing to be. You owe it to your family to stick by them. Think of all that was done for you when you were a little boy, and then growing up.'

'For most of that time,' I told him, 'I was boarded out.'

'Pardon me?'

'They sent me away from home.'

Paul was, quite plainly, incredulous. He almost took his eyes off the road. 'For sickness?'

'No, no. For education and training.'

There was a long pause before he spoke again. 'Then that was when they lost you,' he said, 'not now.'

As we moved closer to the east end we became aware of great jubilation in the streets and at open doorways and windows. Flags were being waved, bottles tipped back and people were waving and shouting to each other. Paul parked the car near the bottom of the side street at the back entrance to Girard's. When we went up we found the first landing door open and a festive bunch of neighbours gathered in the hallway. I caught sight of Emile in vivacious conversation with Jean-Pierre. He waved us in. A wine glass was thrust into my hand and someone else filled it.

I shouted to Emile, 'What's happening?'

He dragged me towards Jean-Pierre's room where a television news programme was just beginning. Several other people bundled in behind me, anxious to see again what they'd already seen. Emile grabbed my arm and declared, 'It is President de Gaulle – he has set the province alight. Nothing ever will be the same again! Look!'

It soon became clear that at a formal dinner in the city earlier that evening the President of France had openly flouted the integrity of the sovereign state of Canada whose guest he was. In his peroration he had loudly declaimed the rallying cry of the separatists, *'Vive le Québec Libre!'*

The shock waves of that spread overnight through the rest of Canada. The federal government was amazed, affronted and furious. The remainder of the visit was cancelled. De Gaulle held on for another day in Montreal where he made a brisk tour of Expo while the crisis grew and roared around him, then he flew back to France.

TWELVE

As soon as I was free of any need for caution or concealment, and was once again in possession of my passport, I took a job. An agency ambiguously called Technical Overload took me on as a piping draughtsman. They employed me and hired me out to offices which needed temporary help. So, I started getting up early and having breakfast with 'the workers'. The duty roster was scrapped. From a bus stop near the digs I had a short journey to whichever assignment I'd been given by the Overload office. Most of them fell within the main industrial area in the east end and lasted from a few days to a couple of weeks.

At the bus stop each morning I saw Yvette. She worked as a secretary somewhere further west. It was only after we'd bumped into each other at the corner of the building where we both lived that we started talking as we waited for the bus. She had a very sympathetic voice and manner of listening. It was as though, whatever I told her, I wasn't telling her half of it, and she considered me very brave for being so reticent. Consequently I found myself talking far too much, at the bus stop and sitting beside her in the bus. Close up, she did look the thirty-five that Hugh claimed she was. Her complexion was very pale and her hair black. Her skin had an over-fine and easily rumpled texture. Her make-up was concentrated around her pale blue eyes.

'But what sort of a *person* is she?' Hugh echoed when I told him about my new travelling companion.

'You should know by now. You've been in there several times.'

'Don't be coarse,' he said, imitating my voice.

'No. Apart from that, you must have formed some opinion about her.'

'A concern masel' wi' very little apart fae "that". But it seems tae me she's a lonely wee woman that happens tae be hooked on a particular pain-killer. An' every man has one.' He averted his head and added, 'Though some in better condition than others.'

Now that I was no longer a fugitive, was earning money and had started on a completely new book, Hugh expected me to report an immediate return of potency. That there was absolutely no sign of such a return seemed to worry him more than it worried me. Once or twice he brought in some mildly pornographic magazines from the cigar-store which did nothing for me but caused him to stand up rather suddenly and ease his underpants. With commendable self-denial he also enquired in drug-stores for likely douches and medications which might alleviate my condition. He knew *I* would never ask for such things but insisted on my using them at least once. It was as much as I could do to escape his personal supervision when I did try them.

But all of that was wiped from his mind early in August. I received a 'phone call during the lunch-break at the office in which I was then working. It was the agency and they'd had a call from a Mr Hugh Gillespie who must see me within the hour at . . . the agency telephonist paused in order to quote the named location correctly . . . at the 'English Brackets British' on a matter of great importance. I smiled at Hugh's way of concealing from my employer that I'd be having an afternoon off for a jaunt to Expo, and confirmed that I would go there immediately.

Despite the heat, Hugh was pacing to and fro in front of the British pavilion, pausing at the end of each patrol to scan the faces passing on the concourse. He ran down the steps as he saw me approach. Gripping both my arms he said in a rush, 'I saw him! On the monorail. Just about an hour ago. And don't for Christ's sake ask me if A'm sure, because A'm sure!'

I nodded and asked, 'Where?'

He pointed. 'A wis up there lookin' directly across at the monorail.'

I followed the line of his finger which described a shallow angle from the top of the French pavilion across the main walkway to the monorail which at that point was raised about fifteen or twenty feet off the ground. Certainly that afforded an unimpeded view at a range close enough to be sure. 'What's to be done?'

Hugh urged me up the steps to the vantage point in front of the British pavilion, talking as we moved. 'A 'phoned Paul as well. He said he'd pick up Emile. Wi' four of us, two can watch the main exit, one can watch the Metro exit and the other can go across to the exit on the Jacques Cartier bridge.' He looked at me anxiously, 'What d'ye think, Bill?'

'That would be best. He'll be off the monorail by now and there's no point in just walking through the crowds. What was he wearing?'

'Dark blue slacks and a light blue shirt but . . .'

'That won't help much. An awful lot of . . .'

He stopped me with an eager, impatient gesture. 'Aye! Listen! It was a *British* casual shirt. Long sleeves rolled up – and nae pocket!'

He was obviously pleased with that definitive piece of observation, and had every right to be. As could be seen from the examples passing before us and all around us: Canadian and American casual shirts, whatever their colour or pattern, all had sleeves that ended above the elbow and an obligatory square breast pocket. Of course Sam would not be the only exception, but even dealing with exceptions was a heartening reduction in the odds against identifying him. Hugh had already schooled all of us on the main description. We would be looking for a man in his early thirties, about six foot, slim build with fair to blond hair. We'd also studied the photograph Hugh kept and which demonstrated that even from the front he looked quite a lot like me. His eyes, though – Hugh had commented – were blue, not brown and in the summer he did not take on a tan but merely got red.

When the others arrived and were briefed on the situation we split up. Emile volunteered to take the outermost position at the auxiliary exit branching onto the Jacques Cartier bridge. Paul

took the Metro exit. Hugh and I manned the long array of
turnstiles at the surface rail link which was quite close to the
British pavilion. There we had the welcome shade of the long
white and yellow striped awning.

For a long time – in the early afternoon – all we had to watch
were crowds coming in. Hardly anyone was leaving so we
relaxed our fixed positions at each end of the long line of gates
and fraternised in lulls between train arrivals. Before long Hugh
came upon the idea of 'phoning the producer of the Paul Reid
radio show. The arrangement was for a brief mention every
Friday but surely they would not pass up the opportunity of
making immediate mention of an actual sighting. Full of confidence, Hugh headed for the bank of public telephone kiosks
behind the brochure counters. He came back well pleased. 'A've
arranged tae give them a call on the air tonight.'

'From here?'

That hadn't occurred to him. 'Christ! That's right. How can
A dae that if we're here tae closin' time?'

'Get them to record it now! Not talking to Paul Reid, just your
telephone call. They can cut that recording into the programme
tonight – if we don't find him.'

Hugh beamed and slapped my arm. 'Billy, ye're a gem! Ye're
a fuckin' *prince*!' He loaded his pockets with small coins from
the station dispenser and dashed off to give his best.

I, too, was very pleased with my suggestion. A breathless,
on-the-spot report, orchestrated with authentic background
sounds of Expo in motion seemed to me an ideal radio item. I
started patrolling the exit line with a lighter step. But Hugh was
gone a long time and before he returned my euphoria was
dampened by my lack of resistance to hunger. The message
from Hugh had been delivered in the lunch break and I had not
taken time to eat any lunch. Gradually I became aware of the
smells of food that were carried on the hot afternoon air and
wafted through the station. Movement only aggravated my
condition so I stopped pacing up and down. Even so, I was
reached by the lures of hot-dog stands, coffee stands, fresh fruit
trolleys, candy floss and even ice-cream. That was the first time
I realised you can smell ice-cream. All that was available on the

station were fruit pastilles and chocolate bars from vending machines. I stocked up on those.

Hugh came back to say that they'd insisted on three separate takes of the report, but at last were satisfied. He himself was less pleased. 'They kept askin' me tae speak in English!'

I smiled. 'And could you?'

He jabbed me in the chest. 'Watch your gub, china!' He looked me up and down, but particularly below the waist. 'Don't tell me ye've managed it?'

I tapped my trouser pockets which were bulging with bars of confectionery. 'No. Not randy, just hungry.'

'Right. Back tae position,' he said, and we resumed our separate sentry posts.

About four o'clock in the afternoon my stomach informed me that if something substantial was not forthcoming very soon, then cramp and painful wind would ensue.

'Ye should've had somethin' tae eat earlier,' Hugh complained when I told him. 'Now's the time when people are startin' tae *leave*.'

'Not many, yet. I've got time before the first real wave of departures.'

'Okay. But try an' be quick. Keep away fae the restaurants, they'll be crowded. See if ye can get a lump o' cheese some-where. That'll haud ye.'

'What about Paul and Emile? They'll need a break, too, before the rush starts.'

'Christ Almighty!' He stamped a few angry paces away from me. 'Ye've hardly *got* here!'

'We've been here over three hours and I don't know if they had lunch or not. Be reasonable.'

He moved in again, noisily sucking breath between his teeth, then conceded that food might be worth trying. 'Okay. When ye've had somethin' tae eat, you spell each o' them in turn. Then come back here. Before five o'clock!'

'I'll try.'

I ran down the steps and followed my nose to the nearest

hamburger stall. There was a queue, or more precisely a mob of little boys on an outing. I waded through them. It didn't matter that they were first, I was taller. Having filled both hands I stopped off to tell Paul of our leader's plans to provision the troops. He gallantly agreed to hold the Metro fort while I travelled to the far end of the island to succour Emile at his post overlooking 'Pioneerland'. To reduce the time involved I took a seat in a brightly decorated electric buggy which travelled along the broad riverside drive around Ile Sainte-Hélène. Between the huge translucent sphere of the American pavilion which glowed green in the sunlight and the sprawling wonders of 'Children's World' there was a wide area of parkland on which a number of family picnics were spread under the trees. The electric buggy, rather like an enlarged and festive golf-cart, hummed quietly along the gleaming black ribbon of tarmac. We passed several men walking along the verge and I took off my sunglasses so that the colour of their clothes wouldn't be distorted. When we passed them I stared back at them and, one after another, they waved.

My journey wasn't necessary. Emile was chattering to a group of local urchins who'd gathered at the exit point to collect brochures and souvenir programmes from visitors leaving the site. They did this with a view to reselling the material to other visitors at the entrance. Emile was augmenting their income by recruiting them as waiters. He wasn't short of food but he was running short of money. I helped him out and hurried back through the bustling, straggling, chattering, laughing obstacle course of brightly clothed crowds to relieve Paul. The people kept moving in odd tangential paths and stopping suddenly to create dense floral-printed, candy-striped barricades. There was a profusion of cameras being incessantly used. In my hurried passage through the busier parts of the fair I must have made an impression on a score of different photographs as I moved in, or just out, or bang in the middle of the shot. I was obsessed by the nagging thought that when those photographs were developed one of them would show, in the background, Sam Hanson and I passing each other. The hot air was alive with a jumble of languages and, on the roofs of one or two pavilions, bands in national costume played loud national music.

The Metro exit was easier to keep tabs on, but even there the sheer variety and constantly shifting patterns of people seemed to defy any effort to concentrate on one particular person. I kept reminding myself – dark blue slacks, light blue shirt, no pocket. But Hugh hadn't told us if Sam was alone. That, I now realised, would simplify matters a great deal. Most of the men were clearly members of families, or husbands, or boyfriends. There were very few men on their own; and those there were seemed to be in the middle-aged to elderly group.

Paul took his time. Not for him the snatched hot-dog or sandwich. Ignoring the deadline I'd been given, he decided that if he was going to eat he was going to sit down and let it do him good. But he was thoughtful, too. When he'd finished his meal he 'phoned Madame Girard and told her we wouldn't be in for dinner. 'She wasn't happy,' he reported.

'Perhaps she thinks we'll claim a rebate.'

This seemed to worry him. 'Ah! I should have told her we would not.' He gave me a questioning look. 'Shall we?'

I laughed and shook my head. Paul, absolved of this oversight in his usually meticulous dealings, resumed his watching stance.

On my way back to the main exit I bought a couple of hamburgers and two soft drink cans for Hugh. As I approached him he extended his wrist and with a rigid finger of his other hand pointed at the damning dial of his watch. I flourished the peace offering of food which he managed to accept without acknowledging it. I asked him, 'When you saw him, was Sam alone?'

He gave me a puzzled upward look over the top of the hamburger roll. Evidently, that was a question he had not thought would arise. It was his assumption that Sam must, necessarily, be alone. He nodded, but now that I'd sown the doubt he did not make it a very convincing nod.

'Was there anyone else in the monorail coach?' I persisted.

'A don't think so.'

'Surely you could see!'

'A wisnae lookin' at anybody else.'

'It's likely that he would marry, isn't it?'

'Nae mair likely than that A would.'

My attempt merely to aid our surveillance had obviously revealed a major hazard to Hugh's whole enterprise. I let him finish his snack in peace. The first wave of departures had begun.

By about seven-thirty in the evening the tide of people began flowing inward once more. Hugh and I slumped together on a corner of the platform to rest our legs. But the mental and visual strain of being so long on the alert was greater than the physical tiredness. If we were going to stay there until closing time we wouldn't be able to stand, or think, or see. Besides, there was a common-sense argument for calling off the guard, though I hesitated to mention it. That would mean admitting we'd failed in this marvellous chance. I began by asking, 'What time was it when you saw him?'

'About one o'clock. How?'

'And you think . . .' I quickly corrected it '. . . we think he'd just arrived then.'

'Aye.'

'So, if he had just arrived on the site at one o'clock and it's now after seven o'clock . . .'

'What are ye talkin' aboot?' Hugh interrupted impatiently – knowing very well what I was talking about, and the likely conclusions.

'That would mean he has spent more than six hours here.'

'Well? So have we!'

'But *he* isn't looking for anybody.'

Hugh scrambled to his feet. 'If you've had enough, Bill, you jist bugger off!' He glared down at me.

'On the other hand,' I continued, not looking up, 'he may have spent a couple of hours on the site *before* you saw him. That would make eight hours, solid. Very tiring.'

Hugh paced about for a few minutes apparently scrutinising visitors but really, I knew, cooling down and coming to terms with what I'd said. I waited, still sitting on the platform and with my chin resting on my hunched-up knees. Eventually he strolled back, and when he was within conversational distance, I offered him a reprieve.

'There's also the fact that you ought to be at the digs where CJAD can reach you if that item gets an immediate response.'

He reacted as though this alone changed his mind. 'Ye're right. We should get back before the show starts.' He looked at his watch. 'Would you tell Paul tae collect Emile, then we'll get a taxi at the harbour.'

It must have been difficult for him abandoning the best chance we were ever likely to have. And there was, too, the painful limiting factor of Sam's being there that day. It reduced all the time we had to a notional two-week vacation period which, as far as we knew, for Sam could just be starting or just ending. At best, the second half of August and the whole of September were emptied of their potential.

There was no difficulty about getting into a taxi at the Cité du Havre end of the Expo express. The difficulty was in getting the taxi to move anywhere, even though its clock was running. Hordes of incoming buses, coaches, taxis and private cars blocked the roads in the older part of the city. We could not have chosen a busier time to be moving in the wrong direction. When the Paul Reid show was due to start we had scarcely progressed half a mile. Hugh asked the taxi driver to tune his radio to CJAD but was told that the driver was obliged to stay tuned to his Control. Hugh paid him for his company if nothing else and we got out to catch a bus which had higher priority on the road.

When we reached the first landing of the digs we could hear the radio going strong in Paul's room and joined Emile there. They reported that the item hadn't yet been broadcast so we all moved along to the more spacious bleakness of room five.

We got through several beers apiece listening to the gentle melodic music that made up the bulk of the programme. And, of course, we heard the current favourite of the channel, Charles Aznavour singing 'If You Go Away'. By the time the crackle of the Expo express introduced Hugh's voice we were all a bit woozy from the combination of exhaustion and the drinks on our empty stomachs. But we were impressed. The description of the wanted man gliding past, unaware and out of reach on the monorail was good. So was the brief sketch of how those islands and the people looked that day. What struck me most was the way in which Hugh converted what could have seemed an indefinable quest into a sharp, practical search. Other listeners could well have formed the opinion that this Sam Hanson was a crucial defence witness in a legal battle of some importance.

There followed the teeth-on-edge snatch of 'Scotland The Brave' then, incongruously, Peggy Lee singing a rainbow. But at the end of that we were told there was a caller on the line and a voice said, 'I am Sam Hanson.' We looked at Hugh who was staring at the black-cased, chrome-bound, portable radio as if it had started to expand. Paul Reid asked a few questions and the answers did come in a Scottish accent. Hugh still sat tense but expressionless. Then he murmured to himself, 'Ask him about Donny. Ask him if he has a brother called Donny.'

Paul Reid announced that the station was now putting a call through to Hugh Gillespie. And it was just by way of padding until the connection was made that he asked his caller about the brother called Donny. The man did not have a brother of that name. In fact he did not have a brother at all. Our 'phone rang and Emile leapt up to answer it. Hugh stopped him. 'No!' He was staring at a spot on the floor between his feet. 'Let it ring,' he said.

The radio programme continued. The caller who had no brother was more than a little offended at finding himself dismissed from the broadcast. He had an interesting story to tell and wanted to know why they wouldn't let him tell it. Paul Reid was still trying to get rid of the man when Hugh switched off the radio. None of us dared say anything for several minutes and there was a great deal of reaching for beer bottles and holding them up to see which ones still had something left.

Hugh started gathering up the empties. 'A think we should all go out an' have a square meal,' he said.

I was the first to agree but Emile delayed us by asking about Donny. 'Is he a younger brother of Sam?'

Hugh nodded. 'Oh, aye. An' mair trouble than he was worth.'

'Maybe it would be easier to find *him*,' Emile suggested.

Paul declared the subject closed for the moment. 'One brother is enough to find. Let's go eat. On me.'

We got into the big green Oldsmobile and drove a long way uphill. The upholstery was still warm from the day-long exposure in the sun-trap parking lot. Paul had decided on a 'decent' restaurant, by which he meant an Italian restaurant. This one, he told us, did a special *lasagne al forno*. It had an open air patio under a scarlet awning. From there we could look down towards the river and, just on the edge of the heat-haze three or four miles distant, we could see the Expo islands sparkling on the dark water like beautifully matched, crescent-shaped jewels held together by diamond threads. Further down the hill in one of the private villas, and hidden by the trees, an alfresco party was in progress. We could faintly hear their laughter and their repeated selection of the plaintive but undoubted hit song, 'Inch Allah'.

It took a long time for Hugh to give even the appearance of having got over the frustrations and disappointments of the day. But gradually he did. Paul and Emile kept up an unforced, amused and amusing conversation. They chose their subjects ostensibly at random and imperceptibly drew the Scotsman into their act. Paul, of course, was the host and he was properly conscious of the fact. He was also, he clearly realised, the ideal 'second banana' to Emile's erratic imagination and off-beat interpretation of even the simplest facts. They were a great combination and I was proud of them that night. With the wine, a sense of comfort and pleasure and peace eddied round our table and imposed the recognition that, whatever had been lost, we four were party to a considerable gain. That's really what Paul and Emile were saying while they spoke of other things.

THIRTEEN

One week after our Expo vigil Hugh's wife arrived in Montreal. He met her at the airport on the Saturday evening and together they booked into a mid-town hotel. All of us at Madame Girard's expressed a keen interest in meeting Moira, and Hugh promised he'd bring her to visit us sometime during the week; probably Tuesday which was a public holiday when we workers would be at leisure. The city observed a great many holidays, or holy days of obligation, because there was a high regard for saints. Tuesday, however, was more important than that. It was the Feast of the Assumption. This posed a slight worry, as I mentioned to Emile, 'Let's hope Yvette doesn't set up any competition.'

'You will see her on Monday. Tell her to cancel the block bookings.'

'We never talk about that.'

'What *do* you talk to her?' Emile wanted to know. 'I would not know what to say.'

'She's just an ordinary, polite, rather timid woman.'

'But surely she knows that we know. She knows you are in this room – and Hugh, which is more.'

'Considerably more,' I agreed. 'However, it seems she has convinced herself that when she turns up the volume on her set nobody knows anything.'

Emile digested the thought. 'We know it is very loud,' he said.

'She could be a deaf virgin.'

Tuesday started cloudy and got steadily worse. The clouds thickened and the heavy yellow tinge on their undersides turned purple. By lunchtime the first thunderstorm rumbled in the clammy air. Without a knock or an apology Jean-Pierre barged into room five and slammed the windows shut. 'Flooding,' he said tersely, 'breaks the ceiling downstairs.' And with that he hurried out to secure all the other windows in the house. I was sceptical of his fears until the cloudburst came. It did not rain like rain. The water came down in solid sheets. The sheer weight of it made the window frames groan. If he hadn't taken action the room would have been flooded in a few minutes. I stared in amazement at the prodigal ferocity of it all while thunder now overhead continued with roar after splitting roar and lightning raked the island from end to end. Occasionally the bell of the telephone down the corridor was jangled by surges of electricity. That was a startling and rather weird sound – an inanimate object protesting at the violence which shook the house. Paul, who was dressed and ready to go and collect the Gillespies, came in and shrugged at the impossibility of trying to drive through such weather.

Emile offered to beat him at chess while he was waiting but he declined. Indeed, it seemed futile to try and do anything while the noise and the torrent continued. I lay on my bed, Emile lay on Hugh's bed and Paul slumped into the armchair. In the middle of the day the room was practically dark.

'I think I know who is behind all this,' murmured Emile to the ceiling, but did not elaborate.

After an hour or so, when the onslaught had dwindled to what in Britain I would have called a downpour, Paul decided his windscreen-wipers were up to it and went out. I switched off the light and went to the window. The streets were running with water but *not* flooded. Unlike British cities which seem to be paralysed even by a heavy dew, the public utilities of Montreal were marvellously efficient. I'd noticed it before when arctic ice and several feet of snow were the hazards. It did not surprise them that the weather was capable of extremes. They prepared and coped and everything ran normally.

*   *   *

'My! That was quite a storm, wasn't it?' Moira said as Paul ushered her in. She was holding a plastic hair-cover at arm's length and her coat had been drenched even by the short walk from where the car was parked. She was a very attractive woman with alert, smiling eyes and beautifully even white teeth. When Emile helped her take off her coat I noted that she had a fullish well-proportioned figure and a tiny waist. When Hugh had introduced us she looked around. 'Oh, it *is* a big room.' Her amused glance to me indicated she was aware that that was all that could be said for it.

While Paul busied himself with the wine bottle at the desk which was set with the half-dozen glasses we'd borrowed from Madame Girard, it was Emile who felt obliged to promote conversation. 'We spend a lot of time here and do not give Hugh much peace.'

'Why is that?' Moira asked.

'Because they're parasites,' Hugh grunted.

His wife pursued the point. 'Are your own rooms . . . worse?'

'They are smaller and worse,' Emile assured her.

'Take a seat,' said Hugh pointing to the armchair.

'We have to take it in turns to sit there,' Paul observed as he poured the wine.

Emile ceremonially escorted Moira across the room. 'You see,' he explained, 'it has the back for pressing trousers.'

'Oh?'

'Yes. Hugh lays his trousers across the back smooth and I lean on it to keep the crease.'

'We all do,' laughed Paul. 'It means Hugh has very keen trousers.'

'Oh, God!' the Scotsman groaned peevishly. 'That's aboot enough o' the domestic details, is it no'?'

I asked, 'Did you have a good flight, Moira?'

'Yes. It was an odd feeling to arrive at practically the same time as I left.'

'BOAC was it?'

'Yes. But I suppose they all do it, flying in this direction,' she smiled.

There was no denying that, and I could not think of any further remarks to cover the awkward pause that was developing. The wine was poured but Paul was not handing it out. He stood at the desk, smiling in an interested way and looking at me. Strictly speaking, and by his instinctive protocol, I was the host. Hugh was lounging on the end of his bed. I took a glass of wine to Moira and indicated that the others should help themselves. Then, feeling quite foolish, I raised my glass and said, 'Welcome to Canada.'

'We hope you will be happy here,' Emile added quickly.

Moira nodded to each of us in turn, 'Thank you. But two weeks is hardly enough time to be unhappy.' She sipped the wine and, aware of the formality that was being imposed on the situation, added a toast of her own, 'May all of you get safe home.'

'That's a funny thing tae say,' Hugh commented as we others found seats where we could.

Emile, her principal supporter, disagreed. 'It is a very nice thing to say. We will not be forever in Montreal.'

'But is likely we will be many other places before we go home,' Paul added.

'A'll drink tae that!' Hugh said loudly, and did so.

'For me, anyway,' Paul went on, 'the next move is to the States.'

This came as a surprise to all of us. We knew of the possibility and had discussed together the pros and cons of Paul's search for higher status. Certainly accepting a job in the States would give him that, and a bonus to take back to Italy. But there was the no less likely possibility of his being drafted into the US Army, unless he was engaged on a job which the Government considered to be of service to the nation.

Hugh did not conceal his irritation. 'When the hell did ye decide aboot that?'

'Hugh!' His wife reacted with astonishment at what she heard as impertinence but which we knew to be genuine concern.

Paul shrugged apologetically. 'It was a sudden decision. They wanted an answer quickly. And it is a very good opportunity.'

'Listed work?' Hugh asked sharply.

'What about Hélène?' Emile wanted to know.

Paul looked from one to the other and suggested, 'Maybe now is not a good time to discuss this.'

Hugh got to his feet. 'A'm no' discussin' it. A'm just askin' if it's listed work.'

'Not to begin,' Paul conceded, 'but soon I could move to a listed project.'

The Scotsman started pacing about. 'Meanwhile, they're busy filin' yer army papers.'

'I'm sure Paul knows what he's doing,' Moira said.

'Oh, you're sure, are ye? Ye met 'im for the first time an hour ago but ye're sure he knows what he's doin'.'

'He says it's a very good opportunity,' she insisted. 'If he doesn't take the chance he might regret it.'

'If he gets shipped straight tae bloody Saigon he'll regret it!'

'Don't be ridiculous. They're offering him a job.'

'Oh, sure! A job where he can spend his *holidays* in the Gulf o' *Tonkin*!'

'Hugh,' I said, 'maybe Paul thinks it's worth taking a chance. If things don't work out right he can always go home.'

'Yes,' Paul said, then with some asperity added, 'but at the minute I am right here.'

Hugh paused in mid-swing between the window and the door, suddenly aware that the evidence of his concern had become presumptuous. 'Yeah. A'm sorry, Paul.' He retreated to sit further from us on his bed.

I took up the wine bottle and topped up the glasses.

'And what do you plan to do, Emile?' Moira asked.

'I do not plan, Madame. I will work and make money and be me.'

'But when you settle down, I mean.'

'Oooh! "Settle down",' Hugh echoed *sotto voce*, but we ignored it.

Emile responded warmly, 'Ah, when I settle down I will get married and have a lot of children. I mean my wife will have them if *she* is settled down at the time.'

Moira chuckled. 'If she's going to have a lot of children she'd better be.' She turned to me. 'And you, Bill?'

'I've just stopped being settled down,' I told her.

Hugh gave an appreciative whoop.

His wife's attentive look wavered only a fraction. 'I don't understand,' she said.

'Well, you see, until now my life was settled in advance, by other people, for me.'

'Surely not! You're a writer. You can do as you please.'

It was *my* turn to be embarrassed. I'd assumed that Hugh would have told her at least some of the facts in my case. But of course he had not divulged any confidential information. 'Ah, yes. But my education and training,' I mumbled vaguely.

Hugh came to my rescue. 'What he means is that he's never had the chance tae be a yobbo like me.'

'Did you want to be?' she asked me with well-simulated earnestness.

'I've never been that ambitious.'

Her friendly but keen eyes crinkled with amusement, though she knew she was being excluded from something. For a moment I thought that that should not be necessary. Yet it was inevitable. Even if she'd spent with us all the time we'd spent together and acquired all the information we thought important, she would have reached different conclusions about it than those we acted upon. I tried to apply her terms. 'Do *you* have a job?'

'Oh, yes! I'm a secretary in an accountants' office.'

'Was that what you wanted to do?'

'Certainly not!' she laughed. 'That's just what was available.'

'But you don't mind.'

'What would be the point?' Moira asked. Failing a ready reply from me upon that, she turned her attention to the charts by the window. She stood up and moved to examine them more closely.

Emile leapt in to explain. 'This is mainly my job to keep a record of all the crimes they do in Montreal.'

Moira scanned the categories. 'They seem to keep very busy.'

'Explosions are best. Then fires.'

'Best? Why is that?'

'For many people can be interested and see them. Or hear them. Robbery and murder are very secret. Unless for "multiple killing", of course.'

Moira gazed at the young Frenchman in some perplexity. 'Yes, of course. I'd never thought of crime as a spectator sport, though.' She turned her attention to our wall-calendar duty roster. 'And what is this one for?'

'That was to wait for . . .' Emile stopped abruptly. He knew this was something which should not be told to everyone but he did not know if it was something which must not be told to Hugh's wife. He leaned forward and ran his finger over the entries as though he himself had forgotten why they were there.

Paul and I concentrated our attention on Hugh, willing him to say something.

He spoke with almost lazy disinterest. 'It's a calendar we use tae make sure there's always somebody up here keepin' an eye on things.'

Moira turned into the room to receive this information but in doing so could not avoid noticing the strained and rather guilty expression which both Paul and I were displaying.

Hugh continued, 'It wid be easy enough for somebody jist tae walk up here and steal whatever they fancied.'

'I see,' Moira nodded and plainly saw there was nothing worth stealing.

The conversation continued to stumble along, veering between our embarrassment and Hugh's ready annoyance. But we were all impressed by Mrs Gillespie. When she asked an awkward question she knew immediately that she had done so. When she misinterpreted a reply she showed no sign of irritation at being corrected or fobbed off. Throughout, she maintained an affable and confident manner in what must have been, for her, an odd and uncomfortable situation. And by the time they were prepared to leave we could just faintly see how she saw her husband. It was quite different from our view, and tolerant for different reasons.

During Hugh's enforced absence on his second honeymoon I got a lot of work done on the completely new book he'd persuaded me to start. Whether this was because I could now afford to hire a small electric typewriter or because the actual material was interesting, I could not at first decide. The story was set in rural England and dealt with a fanciful youth who was prone to rather fey adventures. Emile liked it enormously and as I sat at the humming machine, trickling out words instead of pounding them, he had to be warned not to read over my shoulder – aloud. He also offered to get Paul to illustrate it for me, 'When he has manage to get rid of poor Hélène.'

For Paul, now that he'd decided he would take the job in the States, was applying great diligence to putting his affairs in order. And the most troublesome affair was his girlfriend at Dorval. She wanted him to marry her so that they could go to the States together. That, she felt would be much better than waiting until he bought a house and then sent for her to get married in the States. Paul's difficulty was in getting her to realise that he had no intention of marrying her at all. Since he was a considerate man he spent a lot of time trying to make that fact emerge gradually.

'Why did you tell her that you planned marriage if you didn't?' I asked.

'I never did!' he protested. 'And she has always known it was just an affair. She has others, as I know for a fact.'

'Then why is she suddenly claiming you as a husband?'

'Because, of the men she has, I am the one who has a job in the States.' He sighed. 'It is not Hélène so much who wants a wedding, it is her family.'

I veered to the other extreme. 'Then why don't you tell them all to go to hell?'

'That would not be a graceful way to leave,' Paul said. 'I like Hélène even though she is trying to trick me. And her family has been kind to me.'

'Yes. For a reason, apparently.'

Paul smiled and shook his head at me as though wondering how I could be so obtuse. 'That does not change the fact that I have been happy with her and with them. They have made me happy. And they do not wish me harm.'

'No, they just want you married to their daughter.'

'Who can blame them!' he said, and laughed. 'But it is really, I think, they want their daughter married to my new job.'

In the face of such knowing gallantry I could only repeat, 'If I were you I'd tell them to go to hell.'

'Bill, if you were me I would not be in this situation.'

When he went back to his own room, having thoughtfully swung the door a few times to create a draught, I did try to understand what he saw as his responsibility in the matter. And I could see that his response was better than mine. What I could not see was *why* that should be so.

Moira Gillespie had said of her holiday in Montreal that two weeks was not long enough to be *un*happy there. That proved over-optimistic. About ten days after her arrival she paid us a very *un*happy second visit.

The day had been fine but, in the evening, mist began to gather and by the time I went to bed there was quite a thick river fog. However it was not the sound of ship sirens and horns that kept me awake. I'd no sooner stretched out than channel ten started broadcasting at full belt. It came on about ten thirty and continued for almost an hour, during which I lay on my back, wide awake, cursing Yvette and whoever her athletic partner might be. Or partners, for decreased volume during commercial breaks (which they did not take) allowed me to make out two male voices. They were having an argument. Then one of them seemed to leave and the normal programme was resumed. Eventually that, too, stopped and I turned over, prepared to sleep.

Almost immediately there was a loud knock on my door and I heard Moira's voice. 'Bill! Bill, is Hugh there?'

I pulled on my trousers and unlocked the door. 'Moira, come in!'

When I put on the light she gave one searching glance of the room then moved dejectedly to the armchair. 'I thought Hugh must be here,' she said.

'No. We haven't seen Hugh since your last visit.'

'I'm sorry. I'm so sorry to disturb you, but there was nowhere else.'

'That's all right. I'm glad you came here if there's something wrong.' She was, I could see, exhausted and frightened. 'Did Hugh say he was coming here?'

'No, no! He didn't say anything. He just didn't come back.'

'When? Some time today?'

She nodded, was about to speak then found that her voice was not under control. She just repeated the nod very positively.

I moved quickly to the little desk where Hugh kept a bottle of whisky lying on its side. She accepted the drink and I let her take a few sips before I asked, 'When did Hugh leave the hotel?'

'Just after lunch . . .' she made a small gesture of dismay '. . . during lunch, really.' I indicated that she should take another sip of whisky and having done that she went on, trying to sound composed, 'We had an argument. He wanted us to go to the Exhibition again. But we'd been there practically all of the previous day, and I felt tired. He got annoyed and just stood up and walked out. I thought he'd be back about . . . Oh!'

I sat on the camp stool so that she wouldn't keep looking up at me – as though to see if I thought she was making a fool of herself.

She explained, 'Hugh is very easily annoyed.'

'Yes, I know. But it doesn't last long.'

'That's why I was sure he'd be back at three or four o'clock, maybe. But he didn't. And he didn't come back for dinner either.'

'Did you take dinner?'

'How could I? How would I sit there by myself eating while he was . . . I couldn't . . . And this is such a dangerous city.'

'I'm sure he's safe enough,' I said quickly. 'But I don't know where.'

'Well, he can't be at the Exhibition all this time.'

I knew that he could be, but did not say so.

Moira looked at her watch. 'It's so late! I stayed in that hotel room until eight o'clock then I came out and started looking for him. Trying to find the places round about that we'd visited, then trying to find this place. All the taxis were going the other way and I'd no idea how the buses ran.'

'Did you come on a bus?'

'Partly, but I've walked a good bit as well. Going round in

circles in the fog. And nobody I asked could help. Or I couldn't understand them.'

'Then you need a rest before we think of doing anything else,' I said.

She nodded and seemed able now to relax a bit in the chair. I gave her some more whisky and poured some for myself; moving away so that she would not detect how uncertain I felt about what should be done. Clearly, if she was going back to the hotel she could not go alone. And all the taxis would again be going the wrong way. Those which came this far east now would be bringing their drivers home. I wondered if Paul had driven out to Dorval that night. But even if he was available perhaps Moira shouldn't or wouldn't want to go back to the hotel. In that case, perhaps she could stay where we were. Emile or Paul would gladly share with me and she could use one of their rooms for the night. On the other hand, surely it would be best for Moira, and Hugh, if the others did not know about this painful visit.

'I think I'd better be getting back now,' she said. 'It would never do if he came in and couldn't find *me*.'

'It would serve him right,' I told her.

She gave a spirited little toss of her head. 'Serving him right won't help matters, though.' Then she suddenly leaned forward and listened. 'Is that him now?'

What she'd heard was the argument starting up again in Yvette's flat, this time without the accompaniment of channel ten. I could feel a section of my forehead freeze and start to sweat at the same time. What if Hugh was in there? What if he was one of the men who'd been arguing? Moira looked at me questioningly, trying to make out where the sound was coming from. 'No,' I said as lightly as I could manage, 'it's the man next door . . . and his wife,' I added quickly. 'They're always arguing.'

'Like Hugh and me.'

The voices grew louder and I realised that I had to get Moira out of the house immediately in case it was Hugh and she was able to make a clear identification. I pulled on a tee-shirt but in my haste could locate only the pair of sandals one of which had a broken strap. 'Let's go down and see if we can get a taxi,' I proposed loudly, and went on hoping to blank out the gathering row next door. 'A lot of taxi drivers live around here but there should be . . .' there were two male voices again and Yvette's voice wailed between them '. . . should be one of them starting the night shift.'

Moira stood up and smiled, more for my benefit than her own satisfaction. 'Don't you bother coming down, Bill. I'll manage.'

I took her arm and urged her to the door. 'I'm coming down. And I'm coming with you.'

As we went downstairs she protested without much conviction. The fog was quite thick and I immediately felt the chill of it. As we walked past the corner of the side street where there was a back entrance to the building I tried to make out Paul's car at the spot where he normally parked it. There were two or three cars but the combination of the fog and the street lights made it impossible to tell if his was one of them. I decided we should wait on the opposite corner so that if Paul did return we would see him.

The warning horns on the river were very loud and persistent. Before long, though, and above those deep reverberations we heard a woman scream. That was followed by doors slamming and wild angry male voices. It came from the back of our building. A window shattered and I knew with alarmed certainty that it was the dining-room window of Girard's. The men were fighting on the stairway which led to Yvette's flat.

As we watched, several things happened almost at the same time. Jean-Pierre ran from the main entrance round the corner and threw open the wicket gate to the back entrance. The back court light came on in a yellow diffuse flood that starkly outlined the black gable corner. Emile emerged on the sidewalk at the main entrance and saw us. He came trotting across the side street with his arms in the air. Before any explanations could be exacted the attention of the three of us was drawn to a man rushing out of the side gate, bawling abuse at his opponent, or rival. He got into his car and with a great screeching of tyres reversed it into the car parked behind him. Then he surged forward but was blocked by a small convoy of dock freighter-trucks on the main road. The second man ran out and threw himself into the car that had been damaged. It leapt forward and slammed into the rear of the first vehicle which slewed round and for a few yards ran along with a passing truck.

Yvette set up a long wailing scream and now we saw that she was in the street wearing only a dressing gown. Her body looked weirdly white. The first man now tried to escape but before he could do so he had to suffer a deafening broadside smash from his pursuer. It was then that Madame Girard herself appeared in headscarf and a heavy long dressing gown. Never before had I seen her move with such decisiveness and formidable energy. She strode to Yvette, grabbed her by the hair and dragged her off the street.

Of course there were many more spectators now than the three of us on the corner. There were people leaning out of windows and others standing at open doorways as well as astonished passers-by. Such was the activity and confusion that we did not notice for several minutes afterwards that Paul had joined us. Without offering any explanation I asked him if he would drive Moira back to her hotel.

As Emile and I climbed upstairs to the top floor he was gleefully re-running, with sound effects and actions, the car rutting we had just seen. When we reached the landing he quite forgot that he'd been in his own room and followed me into mine. He went straight to the window to witness the arrival of the police cars, one of which at once sped off in pursuit of the combatants. Only then did he turn with a bright but puzzled look. 'I thought Hugh was here.'

'Thank God he wasn't,' I said.

'What is wrong?' His expression quickly sobered.

As reassuringly as possible I explained the situation that Moira had found herself in. Emile was not reassured. He appeared to become physically depleted by the news, and as I went on he rolled his head from side to side and murmured, 'Hugh. Oh, Hugh!'

'I expect he'll be in the hotel when she gets back,' I concluded.

'She should not go back!' he said fiercely. 'Today he has deserted his wife to chase . . .' he plucked the word from above his head, '. . . chimères!'

'I think he's done that for a long time,' I said.

'It is wrong. I am partly to blame, but it is wrong.' He shook his head dolefully and walked out of the room. His responsibility for bringing Moira to Montreal weighed heavily upon him. And in the following weeks he spent much less time with me or with Hugh. Clearly, he now knew that '*chimères*' should be chased only by young men who did not have wives.

FOURTEEN

It was not until Moira was safely on her way to Glasgow again and Hugh was back in room five – after his two weeks as a husband – that I found out exactly how he'd spent his absent day. He was at Expo, of course, and he'd seen Sam again. But this time he'd seen him go into a large exhibition hall that had only one exit. It was at the International Trade Centre on the Cité du Havre. The hall for engineering exhibits also housed a lounge and bar where exhibitors could entertain possible buyers of their equipment. But casual visitors and prospective buyers alike went in at one end and came out at the other. It was a strictly one-way flow.

Hugh pointed at the spot on the site-photograph pinned to the wall of our room. 'Right there. Mind A mentioned that right at the outset – the engineers' exhibition.'

'Yes, you did. But Sam was a marine engineer, wasn't he?'

'He started in marine but then he went tae the Uni. and got a BSc. Well, anyhow, A wis quite a distance away when A saw him goin' intae that place and A could see it was pretty packed. So, instead o' followin' him in A went right round the outside and got tae the exit. An' A didnae move fae that spot tae they shut the doors. Christ! A wet masel' rather than move.'

I smiled at this unnecessary detail of his report. 'And you didn't see him come out?'

'He *didnae* come out, A'm tellin' ye! No way.'

'Then it couldn't have been Sam that you saw going in.'

'A'm sure it was. But even if it wisnae – A didnae even see the person A'd thought was him comin' out.'

'What was he wearing this time?'

'A grey suit. A kinda business suit an' a white shirt. That's what made me think he was dressed tae travel an' it must be his last day.'

For that was what had made it imperative that Hugh should not miss the chance. If the first sighting at Expo had been near the start of Sam's visit to Montreal then the second, about two weeks later, must have been near the end of it.

'That's how A couldnae come away fae that spot tae 'phone Moira. A knew for certain that if A jist stood there he would walk out.'

'What did Moira say when you explained?'

He gave me a sharp look and raised his eyebrows before moving away to sit on his bed.

'You did tell her what had happened?' I persisted.

'Nothin' happened.'

'Oh, yes! Something did. You left her alone, in an hotel room, in a strange city, for about twelve hours, worried and frightened.'

He hunched forward, tightening his lips and looked at me under his brows. 'She was safe enough,' he said.

'But she didn't know if *you* were.'

He nodded, 'Aye. A've got intae the habit of no' havin' tae worry aboot anybody waitin' on me.'

'But you must have told her something!'

'No. She didnae ask.' Seeing my bewilderment he explained, 'Y'see, when A wis livin' at home, there was many a time A wis away the whole night efter a row. She'd never gie me the satisfaction o' askin' me where A'd been.' He smiled. 'She's a very strong-minded woman, Moira.'

'But I suppose she told you where she'd been.'

'Only because you 'phoned her in the mornin' tae ask if A wis back. Pity it was me that answered.'

'It was quite a night one way and another.'

'Aye. Poor Evie landed wi' a double bookin', and baith o' them heidbangers by the sound o' it.'

'At least we'll have a lot less noise.'

'And a lot less nooky,' said Hugh wistfully.

                    *   *   *

For the 'double booking' and the stramash which followed it cost Yvette her flat. The morning after, as we sat having breakfast at the boarded-up dining room window, Jean-Pierre reported that she was already packing her things. These, including some pieces of her own furniture, would be collected when she found somewhere else to go. Yvette herself, to my amazement, was at the bus-stop as usual. Apart from slight bruising around one of her eyes she seemed perfectly composed. I marvelled that the pretence she imposed on her life was capable of overlooking a brawl, a broken window and a violent car crash. On the journey into the city centre we did not chat about the weather, exactly, but the effect was just as innocuous. As she told it, she'd been having a little party and things had got a bit noisy. After all, you can't have a party without *noise*. And some people are just naturally quarrelsome. I nodded. Then she suggested that Madame Girard had forgotten what it was like to be young. And the window must have been cracked anyway if a person just had to *lean* against it to break it. Yvette confided all this in a quiet, earnest voice and her small white hands rested one over the other on her lap. It occurred to me that she had related similar such difficulties to other people before. The unbecoming urgency of her present removal was new, though. Other people, when they've decided they don't want parties on the premises, at least have the courtesy to give a person a little notice of the fact. In short, I concluded, she'd been thrown out of better joints than this. Before she moved out of the seat to get off she suddenly turned and shook my hand. Then, as she arched her thin neck to negotiate the footboards of the bus I noted that one of her ear-lobes was badly bitten. From the sidewalk as we drove on, she gave me a sad little smile and a wave.

The last week in August seemed to be devoted entirely to preparations for Paul's departure to Sacramento. And now that the decision had been made, Hugh devoted a great deal of thought and energy to those preparations. He was the only one of us who'd actually lived and worked in the States – World Fairs, New York, Seattle – and was able to give a great deal of

very practical advice. Paul himself was full of vigour and opti-
mism. He had now managed the final break with Hélène, and
without making use of Emile's offer as first reserve replacement
suitor. The young Frenchman complained about being spurned
unheard but Paul told him he should think himself lucky he was
so poor, crazy and undesirable.

Emile, seated at the dinner table, bowed. 'These things are
true,' he said. 'Also, I do not have large, green, old, *old*
Oldsmobile that nobody wants.'

He spoke too soon. Jean-Pierre at once appeared in the kitchen
archway. He was about to speak then decided that his line would
sound better from a nonchalant leaning position. When he'd got
that right he said, 'Hey Paul, you getting rid of your car?'

'Well, I don't think I could drive it all the way to Sacramento.'

'Wouldn't have a chance,' Jean-Pierre pursed his lips reflectively. 'Really is a pretty old car.'

I said, 'Perhaps you know someone who would make a reasonable offer.'

Jean-Pierre levered himself upright and came round to collect
empty plates. 'Nope. Can't say I do.'

'It doesn't matter,' Paul said. With a brand-new Mustang in
sight, the fate of his Oldsmobile didn't bother him. 'Hugh will
drive it to the scrap-yard for me.'

'No, don't do that!' Jean-Pierre's voice had a note of alarm
and he laid down his pile of plates at the end of the table. ''S a
matter of fact I do know a guy might be willing to take it off your
hands.'

'But A'm takin' it aff his hands,' Hugh protested.

Young Girard went quickly on, 'This guy lives out Dorval way
. . . near the airport. He could pick it up from there. 'slong as
he knows exactly when you're leaving.'

We looked at each other with some surprise.

Jean-Pierre, fearing that he was losing whatever obscure
advantage he sought to gain, made a further advance. ''s a matter
of fact, this guy might pay you something for it. A good price,
considering, as long as the papers and gear an' all is left right
there with it.'

But his eagerness had betrayed too much. Hugh suddenly

leapt to his feet, reached across the table and grabbed Jean-Pierre by the shirt-front. 'You're a cunnin' wee bastard aren't ye?' His voice was low enough not to alert Madame Girard but had intensity enough to scare the hell out of her son. 'And what's your cut – when Paul's made his getaway?'

Jean-Pierre had some difficulty replying since his chest was bouncing off Hugh's fist. 'Forget it, Hugh. Chrissakes, forget it!' he said. 'It was just an idea.'

'No' a very good idea,' Hugh told him, releasing his grip.

Jean-Pierre seized up the plates and, holding them very high as a kind of shield, backed into the kitchen.

We all rose from the table and called, *'Merci, Madame.'*

'Bienvenue!'

We paused on the outer landing and Hugh explained that in his opinion Jean-Pierre was trying to acquire a decoy vehicle, probably for a robbery. When we went upstairs he elaborated on the system of 'reverse getaway'. Apparently it meant planning a robbery from the discovery of the abandoned vehicle, backwards. If Jean-Pierre's friend knew when the car would be at the airport and its owner 'escaped' over the border, then the robbery would take place the previous night. A 'witness' planted at the scene would describe to the police not the car which was actually used but the car which was going to be found. And, working further back, on any day before the robbery the robber could reconnoitre the scene of the crime by just walking in to complain that one of their customers – owner of a green Oldsmobile – was blocking his exit from the parking lot. That would establish the registration number and description of the decoy vehicle. Also, that its owner was on the premises at that time. All of this, when put into operation, ensured that police time was taken up in pursuing an entirely innocent person.

'That could have been me,' Paul said.

Hugh nodded. 'Yer new employers wouldnae like that when they got tae hear aboot it.'

'But what happens to the "witness"?' I asked.

'Nothing. Y'see, the trick works because the people that are being hunted stay right where they are. It's the innocent party and the police that move.'

'How do you know all this?'

'From crime reporters. They manage tae wring it oot o' the police, but everybody keeps very quiet about it in case it catches on.'

Paul shook his head. 'That Jean-Pierre! But for you I would have let him do it. I am very grateful.' He wandered back to his own room still pondering over his lucky escape.

As Hugh settled to his typewriter I lay on my bed and tried to identify what it was about the elaborate trick which seemed, somehow, familiar. Or, if not familiar, relevant. I kept running over in my mind what Hugh had said about the 'witness'. The people that are being hunted stay right where they are. That is how they escape. The full significance of that did not strike me until a few weeks later.

Before then, Paul's last day in Montreal arrived. As he was leaving on a morning flight our farewell meal was dinner and, in deference to his palate and patriotism, we took him to the place on the hill where he'd taken us on an earlier occasion. Unfortunately it was raining and we had to eat in the main restaurant instead of the patio. Emile was still formal and reserved in Hugh's company and, apart from that, we all felt rather sad. Nevertheless, it was a very satisfying evening.

With his own future settled Paul wanted to know how far we'd got in preparing for ours. And having drunk a lot both Hugh and I conceded to him more than, until then, we'd been willing to confess to ourselves. For Hugh, his second unsuccessful stake-out at Expo had been fairly conclusive. Sam had been in Montreal but now, probably, had gone home again. Besides, there was very little work left for him in Expo itself. Most of the newsworthy visitors had already made their visits. He'd wait until the end to cover the grand closing, of course, and he'd still keep a regular look-out, but he was already planning other journeys in Europe and maybe in the States.

I reported that there would be very little to show for my year of freedom. Having abandoned the Greenock stories I was now rapidly losing faith in the fey English novel – *and* in my ability as a writer. On top of that I'd even lost what I didn't want. Things might change, of course, but I certainly was not going to face another Montreal winter.

Paul told me, 'Now certainly is the time for you to write to your father.'

'No. Or, certainly not about the business.'

'What else is there for you? The gamble did not pay, so!' He gave a dismissive sweep of his hand.

'But now I'm a person who gambles,' I said. 'And my father does not want a gambler.' It irritated me that words which started so clear in my mind came out a little fuzzy. 'Anyway, it's Hugh's fault.'

'What is?'

'Prudence!' I reminded him.

'Never been a fault o' mine,' he asserted.

'No. But it was you who said it was a *fault*.'

The table was silent for a few moments while we all tried to make sense of this. 'Hung out to dry,' I added unhelpfully. 'You said I was to remember you said that.'

Hugh gave me a long earnest look. 'And so ye have,' he said. 'But why did A say ye were tae remember it?'

'Because of prudence.'

'Tae hell wi' prudence!'

'Exactly!' I turned to Paul with the q.e.d. 'That's why.'

Emile sighed, 'Of course.'

But Paul had been keeping his eye on the target. 'Okay. You are not to be a successful businessman. You are a gambler. But what will you gamble on now?'

It was then that Hugh suggested I should join him as a freelance journalist. Or, rather, it gradually became apparent that that was what he was suggesting.

'A've got stacks o' contacts all over the place,' he assured me, 'and ye'd soon pick up the basics for the job. We'd be a good team. You could dae stuff for the toffee-nosed advertisin' rags an' A'd concentrate on the serious papers that want tae know what's really goin' on.'

Both Emile and Paul were enthusiastic about the idea and in the euphoria of my tipsy condition I wondered why *I* hadn't thought of it.

Hugh warned me. 'Of course journalism's a lot harder than writin' a book.'

'In what way?'

'Well, ye cannae afford tae please yersel. Ye've got tae please other people. And on time.'

'Do you really think I could do it?'

'Sure. As long as ye realise that ye jist live tae fill spaces that other people have made to suit theirsels.'

It did not occur to me then that what he described was exactly the situation from which I'd been trying so hard to escape.

Next morning we drove with Paul to the airport and, in the departure lounge, he insisted on taking photographs. It was entirely by chance that I took a snap of one group and Hugh took the other. Paul promised he would send prints. That done, we confined our conversation to remarks on what was happening at that moment; people passing, snatches of music between announcements, speculation on delays and attention to time. Through all this I considered how lucky Paul was that his decisive year had come early and he'd known exactly what to do with it. Otto, too, had known and had leapt towards it. I glanced at Emile who at that moment was trying valiantly to give the impression of being cheerful and unaffected. He still had several years to go but I made a note that I must soon warn him to start preparing. My trouble and, I suspected, Hugh's was that we were ignorant of the hazard until it was upon us.

Paul's flight was called. He shook hands with Hugh and me and embraced Emile who, suddenly, was quite unashamedly weeping. We watched Paul march down the long ramp to the gate and he didn't look back. On our way out, to my surprise, Hugh checked that his message for Sam was still on the personal message board and replaced it there. Apparently he had not entirely given up hope.

We went with the Oldsmobile to the scrap yard and, though we had to wait for quite a while, saw it lifted into the crusher. This was less a sentimental gesture than a determination that Jean-Pierre's associate would have absolutely no opportunity to rescue it as a decoy. But it was sad to see the trusty old green hulk destroyed. We'd come to cherish it more than its owner had before he was seduced by America and a brand new Mustang.

FIFTEEN

September began with an influx of new people. My former room downstairs was taken by a tall and terribly affable Swede who soon proved to be terribly boring as well. Yvette's self-contained flat was let to a young couple from Toronto who had a tiny fretful baby. Paul's room was occupied by a scrawny middle-aged man who personally reeked of carbolic and generously spread a pall of disinfectant over the whole top floor. Carlo's room reverted to storage space.

In room five the effect of these changes was to increase the feeling of dejection. Even if Hugh had not entirely given up on Sam it was worrying that he seemed intent on grooming me as a sort of replacement. Part of the training was a crash-course on journalism; sub-section, feature articles.

'Yer paragraphs are too bloody *long*, Bill!'

'Oh? They're as long as it takes to make a sensible section of the piece.'

He was indignant. 'But naebody gives a damn aboot that! The sub-editor disnae read them for *sense*. He measures them for *length*. It's the look o' the thing.'

'What does it matter what it looks like, if it's worth reading?'

'Because, if it disnae look right, naebody's gonnae *bother* readin' it. An' another thing – ye've got the hooks for the sub-heads too close thegither.'

This meant I had to take care that obviously striking words which could be plucked out to make sub-headings did not cluster like currants in an ill-mixed pudding. Another oft-repeated injunction was that I must avoid using direct quotes in feature material. Apparently random indents dement sub-editors and waste more space than they're worth.

After a few weeks with my irascible tutor my writing style deteriorated enough to gain grudging approval. 'That's a bit better. At least it sounds as if ye wrote it sittin' on a hard chair and no' lollin' back in a *punt*!'

'I've never been in a punt.'

'Maybe no', but the only people ye've read spent that long in punts they got bed-sores, the bastards.'

And that, really, was what blocked Hugh's full acceptance of me. Not my ineptitude as a journalist but the fact that I'd been too far distanced from him at birth and could never really make up the lost ground. Sam Hanson's great virtue as a witness was that they'd been children, then roaring boys together, fighting their way free of exactly the same circumstances and limitations. And each appearing to become what the other wanted to be enabled the laggard to succeed. Finally, as I understood it, they reflected each other exactly.

'And that was quite a trick,' Hugh said. 'Though he seems tae have learned a few other tricks since then. Disappearin' tricks, mainly.'

I smiled and disagreed. 'No. In a disappearing trick the person is there all the time.'

Hugh tilted his head and took a deep drag of his cigarette before he resumed typing. But I suddenly became mesmerised with what I'd just heard myself say. Gradually, a feeling of excitement gathered at my solar plexus and I realised that somehow that's what I'd known I was going to say when – several weeks earlier – Hugh had been telling us about the 'reverse getaway' stunt. What he'd said then was, 'The ones that are hunted stay right where they are. That's how they escape.' I was on the brink of bursting out with this revelation when I was struck by the rather weary composure of the man busily typing on the end of the bed. He'd had enough disappointments in this particular chase. It would be time enough to tell him my idea when I was absolutely certain.

Next day I went to the engineering exhibition at the Cité du

Havre. At the rep's reception desk I passed myself off as a marine engineer and asked for a list and resumé of exhibitors. There were scores of companies and hundreds of names of sales-team contacts and stand managers. I carried the two thick folders to the lounge, bought a drink and went through the documents line by line. Opposite the entry for Industrial Gas Turbines Corp. (Cleveland – USA) I read, 'Stand Manager – Mr S. A. Hanson.'

At the stand I asked to see the manager. One of the sales team knocked on the door of the little office at the back of the exhibit. The man who came out was short and fat and aged about fifty. 'Mr Hanson?' I asked.

'No, my name's Jack Riordan. What can I do for you?'

'I particularly wanted to see Mr Hanson.'

'Yeah, well Sam's gone back to the States for a couple of weeks. I've taken over for him. What's your outfit, Mr . . . ?'

'Thompson. I'm from Colin Thompson Partners, London.'

'Glad to meet you, Mr Thompson. Come on over.' He led me round the exhibit which featured an exploded section of a turbine rotor case made of moulded plastic as well as a complex analog flow-diagram in coloured lights. Inside the office was very quiet.

'When will Mr Hanson be back?'

Riordan swivelled to glance at the wall-chart behind him. 'Monday 25th,' he said.

'Was he here since the exhibition opened?'

'Near about.' Riordan shook his head with tolerant incredulity. 'Even took a holiday on the spot so that he could spend time seeing the rest of this grown-up Disneyland.'

'It is fascinating, though,' I offered, defensively.

Riordan took a covert look at an alphabetic memorandum on his desk. 'We had Mr Colin Thompson visit with us, back in the Spring,' he noted. 'You following up on that?'

'Not exactly. This is more a social call.' The replacement manager nodded, but clearly the news depleted his zeal. And whereas he was willing to hold his end up in preliminary chit-chat, if that was *all* there was going to be no time should be lost in dropping it either.

'Don't get much time for that around here,' he said flatly.

'I hope there was nothing wrong . . . er . . . I mean, that Mr Hanson had to go back.'

Riordan gave me a blank look. 'How well d'ya know him?'

'Oh, quite well.'

'Then you'll know more about his personal business than I do.'

'I just wondered if it was because of illness.'

'No, no. Nothing like that.' He rose and reached for the door handle. 'Great to see you, Mr Thompson. You keep in touch, now.' He shook my hand and, in shaking it, managed to position me at the open door. Obviously he'd had a lot of practice with freeloaders.

I walked through the long exhibition hall without looking at anything and followed the arrows to the exit at the other end. I noted that there was no pass-door at the exit though there was one at the entrance for the use of the staff. 'A reverse getaway,' I murmured to myself with some satisfaction.

Clutching the information folders I made my way slowly up through the city to the park on Mount Royal. After the fierce heat of mid-year which had disintegrated in thunderstorms and fog we were entering now into the calm, mellow warmth of the Indian summer. I sat on a bench and went through the folders in even more detail. What I was looking for was some record of Mr S. A. Hanson's career, birthplace or education. This time he *had* to be the right one. But even the individual company brochure I'd picked up on the stand was more interested in detailing the product than the personnel.

Nevertheless, my success promoted a new enthusiasm for the quest and a determination to pursue it to a gratifying con-clusion. It was not enough that I should be able to locate Sam or tell Hugh where he would be on Monday 25 September. I must bring him back from the World Fair to that dusty, peeling corner on St Catherine East where the trees were now so dry they smelt of *wood*. I got up and walked with new vigour through the park and through the shadow of the huge metal spar cross which guards the city. As I walked along the smooth red soil paths I visualised the astonishing moment when Sam walked into room five. There, before Hugh's eyes, would be the alter ego he'd pursued for over six years, and the illusion we'd been pursuing on his behalf all through the summer. It was a great pity that Paul would miss it. That moment, I felt, would make up for a great deal; and it would be the only real success of my desertion.

To my mind, there was no difficulty at all in keeping the discovery from Hugh for another ten days or so. But I did try to dissuade him from making any further visits to Expo because I felt, when everything was made clear, allowing him to keep up his mechanical, already hopeless watch was what he'd resent. However my suggestion that he should cut down on the visits only depressed him as further evidence of my belief that it was a lost cause.

'A don't give up as easy as you, Bill,' he told me. 'As long as A'm in wi' a shout, A'll keep at it.' And, indeed, he still kept the advertisement going. Also, when the radio producer had wanted to drop any further mention of the search he'd won the concession of occasional references just to fill unforeseen gaps in the running schedule.

As far as Hugh could judge everything was winding down and, with the decrease in the work he had to do, there followed an increase in his drinking. On quite a few occasions when I came back in the evening he was already drunk and counting only on a large dinner to sober him. To my relief he wasn't a quarrelsome drunk but it did make him rather sentimental, and sometimes embarrassingly demonstrative. Then, too, he was full of plans for our future travels together. But though many of these would be new places to me, I noted that all of them were places he had already been with Sam. And he recalled the girls they'd known, to whom he would introduce me – 'that is, if yer gear's back in good nick.'

'I'm sure it will be,' I said.

He shook his head with drowsy sadness. 'Six months, b'Christ, withoot a blow-through. It's a wonder ye don't bloody-well *explode*.'

'I am feeling a *bit* better.'

'Howd'ye mean?'

'Well . . . less numb, I suppose.'

He lurched sideways out of the armchair and accomplished a little arrested trot in my direction. '"Less numb" isnae worth a *damn*, Bill. D'ye know what A think?'

From my supine position on the bed I looked up at him. 'What?'

He swayed a little. 'A think it suits you fine the wey ye are. Ye're no' tryin'. It disnae bother ye. Seems tae me you'd be perfect in a bloody monast'ry!'

'Even if my paragraphs are enormous?'

He gave a roar of laughter, 'Holy God!' and veered away with such momentum that he fell across his own bed.

One of the last jobs the agency sent me out on was to Vickers Engineering. Coming out at stopping time I thought I recognised a tall, sloping-shouldered figure lumbering along in front of me. The man was moving towards the parking lot and I increased my pace so that I could overtake him before he turned off the main road. And he was Jock Turnbull, the senior apprentice from my time in Greenock. It was as though the eight-year gap and thousands of miles were as nothing. He just stopped and said, 'Hello, Billy. Can I give you a lift?'

As he made the detour from his own way home he told me that he'd emigrated as soon as he finished his national service.

'And how is Helen?' I asked.

'Oh, she's fine.' Jock took his eyes off the lemming rush of cars for a second. 'Fancy you rememberin' her name.'

It was not in the least surprising. I had her name in a notebook and a fair assessment of her character. 'I suppose it was Helen's idea to emigrate.'

He nodded, smiling. 'That's right, it was. And I'm glad she persuaded me. We've got everything we want here.'

'Yes, it's a prosperous country.'

'How about you? Were you not supposed to go into the family business?'

'I was, but I didn't.'

He didn't pursue it; not because of a reluctance to pry but because he wasn't very interested in me or anybody's business but his own. However, there was one piece of information which I felt bound to pursue and when he stopped at my direction I put it to him. 'You remember the labourer we called "Lord Sweatrag"?'

Rather puzzled he nodded, 'Uh huh.'

'It was you that planted the stuff in his locker, wasn't it?'

He was astonished. 'And that's all you want to know about me?'

Instantly I recognised that I'd been remiss. I had not praised his car, or asked about his job, or his house, or their children if they had any – and I could not very well tack them on now. 'Yes,' I said. 'That's all.'

'Okay. Sure. I planted the stuff. What's it matter now?'

'It doesn't matter. If you wait long enough, nothing matters.' I opened the heavily padded door of the car and stepped onto the sidewalk. 'But it might as well be accurate. 'Bye, Jock!'

'See you!' he called, and waved as he drove away.

I ran upstairs, eager to add another piece of information to my record of other people's lives.

As I went in, Hugh was pacing up and down the room. And he did not delay in telling me the cause of his agitation. 'Moira's pregnant,' he said.

And now I did make the right response but to the wrong person. Or certainly at the wrong time. 'Congratulations.'

'A can dae withoot the sarcasm,' he retorted and strode to the desk to pick up and flourish an airmail envelope as though it were a warrant for his arrest. 'An' don't ask me if she's sure. She widnae tell me a thing like that unless she was positive.'

I started stripping for my bath. 'Are you surprised – all things considered?'

'Bill, it's no' a laughin' matter. She had this planned. Likely tanked hersel up wi' fertility pills before she got here.'

'Surely that wouldn't be necessary with a man like you.'

'How was *she* to know *that*?' he bellowed.

I pulled on a dressing gown. 'Then you did have something to do with it?'

He threw his hands up in mock despair. 'A wis *used!*'

'Yes. As a husband.'

Giving me a violent push towards the door he said, 'Away and wash yersel'.'

I went slapping down the gritty corridor, wondering how much of Hugh's reaction was self-maintenance and how much fear. There was also the possibility that he'd certainly been party to providing himself with an escape route. At the time, of course, he could not be sure that a child would be conceived, yet the possibility was there and, however distantly, he could have acknowledged that he might have need of that excuse. And now I recalled my surprise at how quickly he'd given in to Emile's trick which brought Moira over. At the moment, though, he clearly considered it bad news. But I would have good news for him in a few days, if I could wait that long to deliver it. For, as I lay soaking in the enormous bath, it occurred to me that I ought to forego the rather theatrical reunion I'd planned and tell him at once that Sam had been found. I decided that if his spirits hadn't improved after dinner it would be time to play the ace.

What neither Hugh nor I had reckoned upon was Emile's reaction to the news. His relief and delight were almost comic. This was proof that he had not made a terrible mistake in setting up the situation which he felt had gone so wrong. This conquered his disappointment in Hugh for the way in which, as far as he'd seen, Moira had been treated. And, inadvertently, he revealed what seemed to me a charming contention. To Emile, when people who were not married made love that was usually just sex, but when people who were married had sex – that was always love. And he had great faith in love.

After dinner he followed us into room five – something he had not done since Moira's departure. This change in the young Frenchman's attitude had a tonic effect upon Hugh and from his response to it I could see how much he'd minded the loss of Emile's company. And the evening started as so many other happy evenings had started.

'We must go out and celebrate!' Emile announced.

'Yes, of course,' I immediately agreed.

Hugh gave me a covert snarl. But, as always, complied with the general feeling even if he lost sight of the purpose of the celebration while the enjoyment of it lasted. We went to a few bars and to a nightclub where the voice of the girl singer had enough high sweetness and purity of tone to induce levitation. And, curiously, it did produce the beginnings of the nearest physical equivalent in me. I tried to stimulate the effect with even more drink but overdid it.

'Who the hell's Elsie?' Hugh was asking me.

I raised my head with some difficulty to find him leaning over a table which was laden with empty glasses. We were still in the nightclub. 'What?'

'Ye keep on ramblin' aboot Elsie.'

The girl's voice rose once more against a discreet, understated accompaniment. I pointed a fully explanatory finger in roughly that direction.

'No. Her name is Rosa,' I heard Emile say from somewhere away to my left elbow. I just smiled knowingly and got my head down again.

Later, I was led out onto spongy concrete and pushed into an alarmingly unstable taxi which soon came under heavy shell-fire. Certainly I could see fires blazing here and there beyond the whirling tops of the buildings we passed. There were bells and sirens, too, approaching and receding with dizzying rapidity. Finally, with a cool gap between my shirt and the waistband of my trousers, I was pushed onto the street again and aimed at a long flight of stairs which, politely but adamantly, I refused to climb.

In the morning – or Sunday afternoon, to be more precise – Hugh woke me up. 'Wid ye listen tae that!' he protested.

I listened and without difficulty, now that I was awake, detected the cries of a wailing infant from next door. 'Well?'

'It's been shriekin' like that constant for two solid hours.'

'Babies cry,' I assured him. 'It'll be all right.'

I was about to turn over and resume my sleep when Emile came pounding on the door and burst in. He looked hellishly bright and wide-awake and thought nothing of suggesting that we all go out for lunch. Failing that, he offered to bring us some lunch in and forced our nodded approval of that before he would go away.

The infant continued to cry and whereas the volume of sound

was nowhere near as great as channel ten on a good night, it was much more distracting. Very, very gently I managed to drag myself into a sitting position on the bed. Hugh evidently was glad of this sign that he was not alone in the Sunday world of retribution.

'Dae you know how long ye've been sleepin'?' he began accusingly.

'Until five minutes ago?'

'Ye were away long before we left that place last night. What the hell use is it gettin' drunk if ye jist go tae sleep?'

'It was only my legs that were asleep. The rest of me was having a good time.'

'Aye. You an' Elsie. *Who* is Elsie?'

I reached over for one of my notebooks but my co-ordination lagged somewhat and the book tumbled to the floor. 'She's in there,' I said. 'A girl with a beautiful voice.'

'Oh, *her*,' Hugh grunted. He'd read my notes. 'A thought it was somebody real that we were supposed tae look for.'

'She's real.'

'Aye. But no' real enough tae keep the taxi waitin' that long. Ye werenae gonnae budge without her.'

The child next door gathered itself for a really sustained wail before cutting out altogether. The sudden and continuing silence was nerve racking.

Warily Hugh asked, 'D'ye think they've smothered it?'

'No. I think they just fed it, or changed it.'

'A wonder if it's a boy or a girl.'

'Probably,' I said, and allowed myself to slump once more into a sleeping position.

All in, that Sunday was a very short day. But it was the day which saw the undeniable start of my recovery. Before midnight on 26th September life was definitely stirring.

SIXTEEN

I woke very early on Monday morning, even without the alarm. There was a lot of planning to do. While Hugh was still asleep I got out of bed and consulted the wall calendar which though out of use as a strictly observed roster was still used by the three of us as an appointments diary. Emile was down for Karate at 7.30 p.m. and Hugh had a call at the Expo press office at 8.00 p.m. Both would have to be cancelled. Now that I was practically certain that Sam would be calling on us that evening it was necessary to make sure that Hugh would not be out. It was desirable, too, that Emile should not miss the occasion, but I had other duties for him as well. And everything had to be arranged before breakfast. I crept around the room collecting towel and soap then opened and closed the door very carefully.

Before tapping on Emile's door I had to decide if he should be told what was behind my requests. My reluctance to spoil the surprise for him had to be balanced against the advantage of securing his full co-operation. After consideration I decided the most important thing was that Hugh should be available to benefit from the surprise, so Emile must be in on it. I tapped gently on the door and waited. Then I gave a firmer tap. Eventually I had to knock loud enough to wake my room-mate before the dozy young Frenchman opened his door. He saw me, let the door swing wider, and went straight back to bed.

'You must be very tired,' I said.

'This is because *I* was awake all day Sunday. What new must you tell me?'

I indicated that we should talk quietly. This was hard to maintain when I told him of my discovery. He stood up on the bed and gave the springs a thorough pounding – which made as much noise as the delighted shouts he was suppressing. Once that was over we discussed what might be the best method of ensuring that Hugh cancelled his press briefing.

'Suppose, one of us is very sick,' he suggested, sprawling back on the bed, mouth agape and one hand trailing on the floor.

'He'd call a doctor. In fact he might go out to get a doctor.'

Emile recovered. 'We could lock him in.'

'I think that would annoy him.'

'But it would be worth it,' Emile maintained. 'Depending on how long he must wait. When will you see Sam?'

'Sometime this morning. If he is there.'

'So! He will come immediate. We must prepare for lunchtime.'

'No. I'm going to ask him to come in the evening.'

Emile sighed and stared hopefully at the ceiling. 'Maybe Hugh's press meeting will be called off.'

'Yes!' I slapped him on the chest. 'We can make sure it is.' I thought for a moment. 'He'd recognise your voice or mine, but I could get the receptionist at my agency to call him.'

'Will she do this trick?'

'Oh, yes. She'll do it for me.'

With that settled the next thing was to arrange suitable provision for the reunion. Emile agreed that he would go to the liquor-store for a lot of beer and a bottle of whisky – to be stored in his ice-box till ready. We also agreed that we should buy cigarettes since Hugh was always running out of them and our guest might be a heavy smoker.

From next door I was aware of the vibrations of Hugh walking across the floor rather than the sound of his footsteps. 'He's up now. And I should have had a bath. Is there anything else you can think of?'

'If there is I will get it with the rest on my way back from work.'

'Fine.' I went out into the corridor, crept along to the bathroom then loudly walked back into room five where Hugh was awaiting my return. He did not notice anything strange then but at breakfast was sharp enough to detect a difference in our behaviour. And some complicity was apparent.

'You two are up tae somethin',' he said. 'What is it?'

And again I was grateful for Emile's effortless inventiveness. He said, 'At last, we have found Yvette's new address.'

'Oh? But that disnae explain why Bill's excited. Unless . . .' he turned to me '. . . ye've got somethin' tae show for it, at last?'

'I've bought a splint,' I told him.

He smiled and shook his head before resuming the engrossing business of eating breakfast. Whereas he didn't for a moment believe the explanation that was offered he knew that whatever the secret was he'd hear about it in good time.

After breakfast I went down to catch the bus at the usual time and stopped off at the Overload office for some mildly flirtatious chit-chat with the receptionist before recruiting her help. My story was that we were planning a surprise birthday party for a friend and we wanted to make sure he'd be there. She seemed happy enough with that and I waited while she called the top floor number and announced herself as an Expo press office secretary. Apparently Hugh accepted the cancellation and I thanked the girl for her help. The unfortunate thing was that she expected me to invite *her* to the birthday party and was quite hurt when I failed to do so.

As I waited for another bus to take me further west, tension started to grow. Of all the interviews I'd ever presented myself for, the one I sought on Monday 27th filled me with the most physical nervousness and mental apprehension. In an effort to pre-empt disappointment I rehearsed all the things that could prevent it happening at all. I invented a whole host of reasons why Mr Hanson would not be available that morning or any other morning. And there was still the possibility that this Samuel Anthony Hanson was the wrong one. The bus jolted along between warehouses and forgotten old streets. I looked at my watch. I was still far too early and got off around Avenue Papineau where the city changes character. Here the bronze sunlight struck a Montreal of steel and glass skyscrapers, banks, shopping malls, boutiques and acres of pale concrete now glowing pink. The change-over was sudden and always astonishing; like turning a seedy corner of New Orleans and finding yourself in the heart of a strangely *clean* Manhattan. I walked in slow easy stages down towards my first marker which was the high central spire of Notre Dame cathedral.

By the time I got to the International Trade Centre it was decently mid-morning and trade seemed to have fallen off quite a bit. Only two of the engineering exhibition turnstiles were in use. There was nobody at the Gas Turbine stand and I waited a few minutes nerving myself to go and knock on the office door. One of the young salesmen came over from the direction of the lounge and asked if he could help me.

'If it's possible I'd like to see Mr Hanson.'

'No problem. You can join him for coffee.'

He asked my name and led me back to the lounge, and to the table where Sam was sitting alone. Wandering after him in a daze, I just could not believe it might happen that easily. The lounge was heavy with the smell of coffee and cigar smoke.

'Sam, this is Mr Thompson of the London Partners,' the salesman said, and went back to mind the store. Hanson stood up and we shook hands. We seemed to be the same height. He looked very much like his photograph except that he was a lot older, and heavier than I'd expected.

'Sit down, Mr Thompson,' he said. 'Can I offer you some coffee?'

'Thank you.'

'How is Thompson senior?'

'He was very well the last time I saw him.'

'I met him here at a state-of-the-art conference,' Hanson said. 'We got on very well. Of course, I didn't know then that he was looking for a new partner.' Hanson had a relaxed voice and an American accent which blanked out all Scottish sounds except the tenacious "r". 'I suppose that is the reason for your visit?'

So attentive had I been to the sound of his voice that I'd missed what he was saying with it. 'I'm sorry?'

'I was talking about the advertisement – inviting applications for a junior partnership with your father's company.'

'I didn't know about that.'

Hanson was slyly sceptical. 'Really? It *is* in all the trade papers, Mr Thompson.'

'Nevertheless.' And I was thinking that of course that's where Hugh should have advertised, in the trade papers.

Hanson continued in an urbane manner that sought to balance my avowed ignorance against his better judgment. 'And I suppose you don't know, either, that I have applied.'

I sipped my coffee with a mechanical regularity, waiting for the first opportunity to state *my* business. 'No, I didn't know that either.'

He lifted his cup off the table and leaned back on the glossy black cushion. Obviously my cagily assumed ignorance of his prospects was beginning to unsettle him, but while he was working out the next tactic he kept a smile on his face. He could, I noted, swallow coffee without losing the smile. 'Colin Thompson Partners is a fine outfit,' he said. 'And I must say I was impressed by your father. Very quiet, but very strong.'

Only peripherally did it reach me that I was being soft-soaped by a smooth operator. Vaguely I tried to locate what was wrong with what he was saying. Possibly it was that he thought I was important as well as being of some potential use to him. And neither of these things was true.

'I'm a friend of Hugh Gillespie,' I said abruptly.

He rocked forward. 'Hugh? Hughie Gillespie! Is he in London now?'

'No. He's here. In Montreal, I mean.' And at that moment I felt the first fine sliver of ice pierce the warm certainty I'd brought with me. It was not that the expression on Hanson's face markedly altered. The smile went on. But his alert blue eyes suddenly gave the impression of being *held* open in pleased astonishment. I went on, 'He and I share digs out in the east end.'

'Well! That is a surprise. I haven't seen Hughie for . . . Oh, it must be . . .'

'Eight years.'

'That's *right*! When he got married. Is Moira out here, too?'

'No.'

He nodded, partly to acknowledge that that would have been

unlikely and partly as a carry-over from his 'well-it's-a-small-world' reaction.

'How's your brother?' I asked.

His eyes scanned me warily. 'Fine, thanks.' He gave a cool chuckle. 'Hughie must have told you quite a bit about me. Though I'm surprised he mentioned Donny.'

'Why?'

Hanson shrugged and made a tight regretful grimace. 'To say the least, they didn't get on very well.'

'So I believe. But he *is* your brother.'

He affected a hearty laugh. 'Mr Thompson, the things you don't know and the things you do know just don't add up.'

'I'm sorry. We seem to be at cross purposes.'

'You are from the company of Colin Thompson?'

'No. I am his son. But I'm not in the company.'

'Let's start again. What was it you particularly wanted to see me about? Riordan left a note for me . . . and here you are again.'

But the ice had thickened and I faltered. 'I just wanted . . . er, to suggest that you might like to visit Hugh.'

'Sure! Of course, I'd like to. But there isn't going to be much time for social calls. There's an awful lot involved in packing up this circus and I've got less than a week now.'

His gesture swept in the direction of the stand but managed to encompass much more than that. I stared at the line of brightly decorated displays and wondered how I could salvage something. 'I believe you went to a lot of World Fairs with Hugh,' I said, and felt as though I was trying to right a derailed locomotive with a toothpick.

'A great many,' Hanson said. 'And we had some great times, too.'

'And how do you rate this one?'

'It's the best I've seen. And I knew it would be. That's why I got the company to assign me to the stand.' He levered himself out of the chair, 'Talking of which – I'd better get back to it.'

I remained seated and reluctant to abandon the slight glimmer of hope. I asked him, 'Don't you wish you were still free to enjoy the great times you used to have?'

He straightened his stylish waistcoat and looked at me with amused perplexity. 'No. What's gone is gone.'

As he was about to shake hands with me I ignored the gesture and delayed his escape. 'Don't you think it might be worth just a little effort to recapture it?' I felt wretched at placing myself in the position of virtually pleading for Hugh.

Hanson barely tried to give the impression that he was considering the question. 'All my effort,' he said, 'is aimed at the future. New plans, new projects . . .'

'New people,' I said.

He nodded conclusively and leaned across the table to seize my hand. 'Goodbye, Mr Thompson. Give my regards to Hughie.'

'Goodbye.'

He'd taken several paces away before he turned to call, 'Here's hoping I see you in London before long.' He waved and disappeared behind a huge clump of indoor plants.

I continued sitting alone at the table for a long time. And eventually I became aware of a most striking irony. I smiled at myself. All during the summer we'd been afraid that Hugh would not find Sam again. What we ought to have feared instead was that he *would* find him.

Eventually I roused myself and went out into the hot mid-day sunlight. Suddenly there was absolutely nothing to do and the whole afternoon was yet to be filled. The Expo site was less crowded now that practically everyone's annual holidays were over. It was possible to get a table for lunch without waiting and I enjoyed a good lunch. But now I deeply regretted that I'd told Emile of my discovery. He felt things more keenly than I and could well have been spared the disappointment.

When I got back to the corner on St Catherine I did not go into the house, because Hugh probably was there already. I waited in the street for Emile to get back from work. I've never been able to explain why the twenty or thirty minutes I spent on the sidewalk then made such an impression on me. Loitering in the warm sunlight at that noisy, littered corner, while house-wives bustled past carrying baskets of fresh vegetables and the children came home from school in laughing, dallying bunches.

Like children anywhere, when they came *home* from school they somehow managed to make their smart, clean clothes look bedraggled. Groups of them divided as they came to me but continued their conversation round me. I felt that if I dug my heel into the dry soil at the base of one of those weary trees, the mark would stay there forever. I kept glancing east and west and at first did not see Emile smiling at me from directly across the road. He was wearing a rather grimy looking yellow shirt and brown oil-stained trousers belted tightly at the waist. He carried a plastic bag in each hand and as he crossed the road through heavy traffic he moved the bags in unison as though they formed a torero's cape by which means he dealt with the trucks and cars which charged upon him.

When he gained safe ground I told him, 'Sam won't be coming.' As usual he was able to tell from my manner, tone and expression much more than the simple statement conveyed. He never required much explanation.

'But you met him.'

'Yes. He has no time to visit Hugh.'

'Today or ever,' Emile stated.

I nodded and for a few minutes we just stood there in the street together watching the traffic pass. 'Of course, I won't tell him,' I said.

'Unless it would help to tell him – to be angry now and forget it.'

I considered that possibility. Emile meant that if I could report that Sam was a phony who detested his former buddy then Hugh might be able to rally against that with his usual combative spirit. 'No,' I decided. 'It's just that he doesn't see things the way Hugh sees them. Perhaps he never did.'

'I cannot believe *that*,' Emile declared stoutly. 'Hugh will not be wrong about how it was in the past. That is certain.' He turned towards the stairway and went up as though the torero's cape had become arm-stretching weights.

Hanson had told me that he was packing up and would be gone by the end of the week. That meant there was still a danger of

Hugh finding him. Even though I'd no intention of giving anything of my discovery away, there was still the possibility of a chance sighting and there was still the advertisement in the *Montreal Star*. Hugh's name wasn't mentioned in that, so Sam might respond to it. Emile and I did our best to lessen the danger by inventing reasons to keep Hugh away from Expo and turning every conversation away from Sam Hanson. We could offer some consolation, though. During that week our Scotsman must have wondered why the beer never ran out, the whisky level held up and he always had more cigarettes than he expected. Emile took great delight in accomplishing these wonders without revealing how they were managed.

I did not tell Hugh, either, about my now revitalized potency because he was sure to insist on a demonstration. It puzzled me that my recovery apparently started on the night I got very drunk – which seemed to run counter to accepted wisdom on such matters. More likely the stress was resolved when I stopped trying to be a person I was not. Whatever the reason, I was very glad of the return to normal service.

Hugh himself was more preoccupied with calculating what could be accomplished in the period of freedom he still possessed until the baby was due. As he saw it that still amounted to a hectic period of activity. He reckoned on the rest of the autumn, the whole of the winter and all of next spring. I pointed out to him that Moira couldn't very well go on working to the moment of delivery. 'Christ, ye're right, Bill. Now, what is it?' He concentrated hard to recall his slight knowledge of the gestation process and came up with a piece of children's doggerel. '"Three months o' pleasure, Three months o' pain, Three months o' swellin', And oot pops a wean".'

'I don't think that's a very safe guide.'

'Maybe no'. When dae you think she'll hivtae stop work?'

'Probably at the end of this year.'

'Aye.' He paused in pacing the room to stare at the letter in his typewriter. He was writing to Moira. 'That puts a damper on *our* plans, eh?'

'I can make other plans,' I assured him.

'Sure! But A promised A'd get ye set up as a flashy foreign correspondent.' He gave me a worried look. 'A hope ye don't mind me sayin' this, Bill . . .'

'I'm sure I shan't.'

'. . . but A don't think ye've got much chance in this gemme withoot me.'

'I don't think I would have had much chance, even with you. I just haven't got the ability. And there's no future in chasing illusions.'

'It's no' ma *fault*, Bill!' he protested.

'No! No, of course it isn't. There's no fault. Just a lack.'

'Does that no' worry ye?'

'No. I'm sorry about it, of course, but I did try and it didn't work.'

'A told ye it widnae.'

I smiled. 'You certainly did. Often.'

'What A should have told ye was tae head straight for the boardroom an' no' waste yer time.'

'I'm sure the time has not been wasted.'

'What is there tae show for it?'

It struck me that he was being purposely obtuse. I protested, 'Surely we have gained something!' But he held his blank, questioning look so I contented myself with adding, 'Most of the time, I have enjoyed being here.'

He shrugged dismissively. 'That's easy enough. It's easy enough tae enjoy livin'. But there's got tae be mair than that, eh?'

'Perhaps. But I'd settle for that.'

'Then ye're easy pleased.' And he found something else to complain of. 'Yer bloody man Otto never showed up either!'

'There's time enough yet.'

'Naw. He's made his jump. He'll no' come back here. Why should he?' At the window, Hugh raised his hand and waved to someone in the street. Immediately afterwards we heard Emile climbing the stairs two at a time then slamming into his own room. The noise woke the baby in the flat next door and it started crying. That was a sound we were used to now.

'So – what *are* ye gonnae dae?' Hugh challenged me.

'I don't know yet.'

'What aboot yer stories, though? Yer notebooks?'

'They'll be no use to me now,' I said. 'You can have them, if you like.'

'Sure. A'd be glad tae have them,' he asserted with more goodwill than conviction. He grinned, 'Maybe A'll take them doon tae Greenock and challenge the buggers tae deny what ye wrote aboot them.'

'Give my regards to Greenock,' I said.

'Sure. But what aboot the other places A could have been tae, that A've never been before? What aboot the people waitin' for me there – in places A'll never see?'

He spoke very seriously and for a moment in the mellow amber light of the late afternoon I could visualise what he feared. Stretching out in what had been his future there must be people waiting: people he would have met, fought with or cared for; people whose lives he would have affected in some way. What were they to do now? Of course there would be other travellers, but there would not be this traveller again. Yet it could be that those who came instead would be more valuable, if only because they did arrive in time. So there was no point in wondering about those unknown and punctual travellers, or about the people who would rather have welcomed Hugh, if they'd been given the chance. Remembering the shiftless osier stringers of San Luis Rey, I said, 'Perhaps they will not need you.'

At the window, facing outward, he stretched his arms to rest on the upper frame. 'A'm no sayin' they *need* me. But there's bound tae be a gap, isn't there?' He drummed his fingers on the pane above his head. 'The same as A feel a gap because Sam couldnae be found.'

For the briefest moment I thought of telling him, but instead suggested, 'Why not put another advertisement in the papers – or give Reuter a communiqué for general release?'

He grunted with amusement. 'Sayin' what?'

'Saying, "To whom it may have concerned – Hugh Gillespie will no longer be able to attend your life."'

He shook his head, quite wrongly assuming that I was mocking him, and returned to the unfinished letter. 'So – what will A tell Moira?'

'Tell her to expect you as soon as the World Fair closes.'

'Might as well,' he said, dragging the camp stool up to the keyboard.

And that was where it ended, though we did wait on until the last fireworks display faded on the St Lawrence. We watched it, Hugh and I, from the deck of the French pavilion. Then he went home to stay and I went back to sea.

ANTHONY POWELL

THE FISHER KING

Anthony Powell's first full-length novel since the completion of
A DANCE TO THE MUSIC OF TIME

An ancient myth refashioned with contemporary characters in a modern setting produces an acknowledged masterpiece.

'His version of The Fisher King becomes an ironic romance, handled with the elegance of a master. And one can only be grateful to hear again the tone of that sharp, exacting Powell voice'

Malcolm Bradbury

'A thoroughly entertaining story . . . cleverly linking the myths of our common past to the humdrum present and casting rich light on both . . . This when you least expect it, is really what makes a great novelist'

David Hughes in The Mail on Sunday

'THE FISHER KING is a rare work of art for a number of reasons . . . Powell is above all funny, and makes humour out of both the gravity and perceptiveness to which narrative aspires . . . I could read whatever Powell writes from here to eternity'

John Bayley in The London Review of Books

'What Powell understands better than any other living British novelist is the importance of selection and emphasis in the telling of a story'

A. S. Byatt in Books and Bookmen

sceptre

Current and forthcoming titles from Sceptre

ANTHONY POWELL

THE FISHER KING

NIGEL HAMILTON

**MONTY: THE MAKING OF A GENERAL
1887–1942**
**MONTY: MASTER OF THE BATTLEFIELD
1942–1944**
**MONTY: THE FIELD-MARSHAL
1944–1976**

WINSTON CHURCHILL

THE RIVER WAR

JOHN COLVILLE

**THE FRINGES OF POWER:
VOLUME TWO**

J. M. O'NEILL

OPEN CUT

BOOKS OF DISTINCTION